MW00748448

ALSO BY MATTHEW REVERT

Basal Ganglia

Before I Die, I Will Build a Windmill

How to Avoid Sex

The Tumours Made Me Interesting

MATTHEW REVERT'S

LEMON HEART

LAZY FASCIST DOUBLE #1

LAZY FASCIST PRESS
PO Box 10065
Portland, OR 97296

www.lazyfascistpress.com

ISBN: 978-1-62105-179-4

Printed in the USA.

LEMON HEART

Matthew Revert

LAZY FASCIST PRESS

Donna behaved the poorest at the most inopportune times. As if sensing the emotional weight and import of a situation, she would pounce with all the ill-mannered intention she could muster. Donna's mother was a timid lemon wedge that slunk through life behind the safety of her husband, never really needing to call upon herself to deal with anything. Her husband passed away some months ago, and since then the impetus had been upon her to handle life's more unfortunate aspects for the first time. As a lemon wedge this would have been difficult enough, as a timid lemon wedge this approached impossibility at sobering velocity. The extent of Donna's intuition (combined with a natural nasty streak) enabled her to sense the despair swimming about her mother and use it against her. On this particular day Donna's nasty streak took the form of defecating into her hand before greeting the town's aristocracy. Polite smiles followed by hearty handshakes followed by recoils in disgust and Donna's work was done. The lemon wedge wept tears of lemon juice while the aristocracy left the party at such a rate that their having been there at all was essentially erased from history. The lemon wedge shuffled to her room, sobbing loudly all the way. Donna remained in the foyer with a glimmer in her eye, making fecal handprints on the wall. This was no way for an intelligent 28-year-old woman to behave.

"You're a nasty, horrible wretch of a daughter," the lemon wedge had said later the same day. The tears had now subsided but if anything the anger had intensified. Donna merely responded in a way that denied the lemon wedge her justified anger.

"Calm down, mumsy. Boy o' boy does my poop stink."

"Yes!" screamed the lemon wedge. "Your poop does indeed stink and now you have it all over my walls and all over the pampered hands of this town's aristocracy. If you have your way, no one here will ever have anything to do with me."

Donna grinned the goofiest of grins, stomped her feet playfully and responded, "I'm a scamp I am," in a poor cockney accent.

"If your father was still here he'd kick you so hard in the cunt…" The lemon wedge scurried away to prepare dinner for her undeserving daughter.

The sounds and smells of tension-heavy cooking filled the air as Donna sat in the lounge room watching television. Television consisted solely of a news story concerning an undefined paper shortage looped 24 hours a day, 7 days a week and had been playing for the last six years. Rumor persisted that the publicized paper shortage had ended mere days after the original story went to air. Donna's familiarity with the story caused her mind to wander into introspective locales. Donna dwelled on the unsavory ways in which she treated her mother. She wasn't sure why she acted as she did. Perhaps, despite every effort made to convince herself otherwise, she really did resent her mother for being a wedge of lemon. Perhaps it was her mother's lack of independence that angered Donna so much. Whatever the cause, there was a distinct impression her actions were largely involuntary and ultimately unavoidable. Unfortunately for both herself and her mother, this was the way it would have to be. Donna glanced toward a family portrait hanging above the fireplace. There they were frozen, smiling as a happy family. Donna's father sat to the right, holding her mother up to the camera in his hand, which was streaked with the juice of his wife. Donna was on the left, smiling eagerly with her arm around her father and a finger gently stroking her mother. Donna failed to recall when the photo was taken, but she remembered the sense of joy that was such a part of her life at the time. The loss of joy didn't coincide with the passing of her father as many assumed, Donna felt an all-pervasive bitterness many years before, which had only gained in intensity. The outward manifestation of this bitterness had been directed at her mother from the start. In the loss of her husband as protector and shield it appeared her mother was unable to acknowledge this. It was much easier to assume Donna was acting out as part of a grieving process. This simply wasn't true however. Donna's grieving process consisted of nothing more than several days of uncontrollable flatulence.

Dinner was an icy affair. The two sat in silence except for the occasional raspberry Donna could not help but blow in her mother's presence.

"Can I squeeze a bit of you on my fish, mum?"

Donna's mother refused to say a word. The only sound in the room emanated from noisy chews on overcooked spinach which pierced the silence like a wet, spongy knife. Donna tilted her head to the side in a faux examination of her mother.

"You look a little dried out. Do you want some cocoa butter? Of course you do. I'll go get you some. Wait here okay, mumsy."

Donna rushed upstairs, deliberately knocking into things as she went. Meanwhile the lemon wedge, so close to the end of her delicate tether, sat alone, silently hoping Donna would never come back downstairs. She envisioned a swirling vortex sucking Donna up and out of her life. She envisioned her husband coming through the front door and embracing her as if back from a long work trip and not from death. The lemon wedge momentarily became lost in the beautiful serenity of her thoughts and, for a few wonderful seconds, forgot the reality of her life. The serenity was shattered by an obnoxious squirt of cocoa butter right in the lemon wedge's face.

"Rub it in, mumsy!" Donna laughed hysterically at the sad sight of her mother lost among the cocoa butter. The lemon wedge could no longer hold back the tears that had been threatening to erupt since preparing dinner.

"You're sourer than me and I'm a lemon."

"Correction mumsy, you're a wedge of lemon."

The anger in the room began to rise as Donna and her mother took opposing stances.

"My comment still stands. You've become a perversion of humanity. You've become evil!"

"Evil? Me? I don't think so, mumsy. You're a disgrace to citrus everywhere. You're weak and you're pathetic. I still have a hard time believing that *somehow* you gave birth to me. Somehow you squeezed me out like rancid juice and here I am. Somehow you managed to reproduce with a human male many times your own size. The logic isn't there is it, mumsy? Can you please explain to me the mechanics of a human/lemon reproductive relationship that results in a fully functional human child?"

"For your information, bitch, I was in labor with you for longer than you'll ever understand and I experienced more pain in that labor than you will ever come close to experiencing in your miserable life. You call me weak? You wouldn't understand the true meaning of strength if it bit your arse off and spat it down your ungrateful throat!"

Donna was mentally preparing to launch into an attack she hoped would put her mother out of argumentative spirits for good when her vision became cloudy. She couldn't tell whether it was her or the room that was spinning. The trickle of blood that leaked from the nostril went unnoticed as Donna passed out. Although by accident, the lemon wedge had the final word, which was enough to convince her of victory.

Ian was a pomegranate who stole children. Although much smaller than those he held captive, he had an immense cunning, which enabled him to lure nearly anyone he pleased into whatever trap he devised. On this particular morning he was positioned on Mr. Whitley's fruit and vegetable cart awaiting Susie's arrival. Susie was a local girl, 10 years of age, who was quite famous in town due to the sole care she took of her sick mother. Susie was excused from school in order to tend to her mother whenever it was necessary. These days it seemed that school was perpetually on the back burner as her mother had taken a nasty turn for the worse, leaving her bedridden and subsumed with melancholia. On Wednesday mornings Susie would venture to Mr. Whitley's fruit and vegetable cart at roughly the same time to buy supplies for the week, which she was destined to prepare, cook and feed to her mother via a juvenile system of tubing and steam valves. As Susie picked her pomegranates it was easy for Ian to subtly roll into her hand and convince her of his perfection as a piece of fruit.

Susie didn't assume for one moment she was holding Ian, the strange pomegranate that lived on the outskirts of town. She was already halfway home when Ian finally spoke up.

"Susie," he whispered in a gruff voice.

It was apparent Susie hadn't heard him over the communal din of the town. He kept repeating her name, slightly louder each time until Susie snapped out of whatever childish daydream she was currently engrossed by. She darted her head about, trying to find the source of the odd, little voice.

"Down here in the basket."

Susie looked down to discover Ian staring back at her.

"Hello," she said with a confused look that was laced with innocence.

"It's me, Ian; Ian the pomegranate. I have a favor to ask of you."

"What are you doing in there, Ian?" Susie asked, seemingly ignoring the mention of the word 'favor.'

"I need you to take me home, Susie. There's been a slight misunderstanding."

"Take you home? I couldn't possibly. Mother's expecting me and if I'm not home within a reasonable timeframe she worries ever so much."

Ian fully expected this initial refusal but remained confident he'd get what he wanted.

"You don't understand Susie. I was walking through town, going about my daily routine when I was accidentally kicked aside by a large man who clearly didn't see me in his path. I rolled along the ground for some time, eventually hitting Mr. Whitley's fruit and vegetable cart rather hard. The pain in my side made it quite impossible to move of my own volition. Seeing me lying there at the base of his cart, Mr. Whitley picked me up, clearly assuming I had fallen and placed me with the other pomegranates. Before I had time to protest he had already moved away to tend to some other business."

Susie had a look of genuine sympathy in her eyes.

"Poor Ian. You must be feeling terribly sore."

She wore a simpering expression, clearly wrestling with the perplexity of the situation as best as a child could. Meanwhile, Ian wore a hopeful expression. The hook was lodged in Susie's throat and he was gently reeling her in.

"Whadya say, Susie? Can you take me home? It really isn't that far."

"Gee I don't know. I'd like to help you, really I would..."

Ian cut her off right there.

"Look, Susie. If you're really worried about your mother I'll write you a note. I'll tell her what a savior you were and even seal the envelope with a fragrant squirt of my juice. You do want to be a savior, don't you Susie?"

Susie stared down at Ian, confliction abounding.

"You won't go away empty-handed Susie. I'll make you up a wonderful hamper full of treats for both yourself and your mother. You'll go to sleep tonight knowing you've done a truly good deed. Imagine if you hadn't been the nice little girl you are. You might have taken a bite right out of me. You've already saved my hide; you might as well take me home and reap the full benefits of your heroism."

The word 'heroism' rang in Susie's ears until, with a resolute air of certainty, she joyfully proclaimed, "I'll do it!"

Ian could barely stifle the grimace as they altered direction and headed toward his home. *Prepare to build some trains, Susie* he thought.

"It really is a most unusual thing," said Dr. Laurentis as he paced backward and forward around Donna's hospital bed.

"Unusual? In what sense?" asked Donna in a groggy syntax.

"We've run all the relevant tests and there's only one logical conclusion, and I'm not sure how *logical* a conclusion it truly is."

"What on earth do you mean? You're making very little sense, and to be completely honest, you're scaring the bloody fuck out of me."

"Well, let me ask you something, Donna, and if you feel it appropriate, I'd ask that you answer with the utmost honesty."

Donna was visibly shaken by Dr. Laurentis's solemnity. Despite a hopeless sense of foreboding she remained a steadfast part of the conversation.

"What do you want to know?" she stammered pathetically.

"Tell me, Donna… have you felt *different* lately?"

"Different? How do you mean?"

"Emotionally? Temperamentally? Have you been acting at all differently toward those around you?"

"I'm not sure. I have to think."

"Well think clearly dammit! I'm in desperate need of the toilet!" Dr. Laurentis yelled in a momentarily undignified way, taking Donna completely by surprise. It made the process of lucid thought all the more difficult.

"Dr. Laurentis, please go to the toilet. Not only will you feel relief but it will enable me the opportunity to gather my thoughts together."

Dr. Laurentis spent some time pondering this suggestion, weighing up the pros and cons before regaining his composure and eventually saying, "Are you sure? I may be a while. I'll be doing a shit."

Donna nodded emphatically and waved him away.

She stared at the hospital ceiling, trying to zero in on the change in attitude Dr. Laurentis suggested must have accompanied the current hospitalization. It was quite obvious to her, even from the moment Dr. Laurentis asked the question, the change in attitude clearly manifested as an unfavorable attitude toward her mother. Donna was almost ashamed to admit this to herself until the ever-familiar urge to act the cad took hold. She passed ferocious gas, instantly blaming it out loud on her mother, despite the fact she was currently alone in the room. Before the smell could dissipate Dr. Laurentis re-entered the room, looking relieved.

"That smells especially unpleasant," he earnestly proclaimed as he fanned his nose with his hand. This led to an awkward silence that felt longer than it actually was.

"Pay it no mind," he continued, trying to alleviate the situation. "Now then, Donna… Have you had a think about what I asked you?"

"I have," she answered.

"Well then, would you say you've been acting differently lately? If so, how?"

"I haven't been a very pleasant person, Dr. Laurentis. I can't pinpoint exactly when it began but I've had a distinctly bitter disposition, especially toward my mother for at least the last couple of years."

Dr. Laurentis took a seat next to the bed and carefully pondered Donna's words.

"Int-er-est-ing," he said using drawn out syllables.

The anticipation was beginning to irritate Donna to a

point where she visualized mashing Dr. Laurentis's genitals in her hands.

"What is it? Can't you just tell me, Dr. Laurentis?"

"Ok, ok. You say you've been feeling a sense of bitterness?"

Donna nodded.

"Rather than bitter, might you call this a 'sour' feeling?"

"I may. Why? What are you trying to say?"

"I'm sorry, Donna. I'm not normally one for beating around the bush but as I said, this really is a most unusual thing."

"What is unusual?"

"Well, Donna... It would appear that your heart, for whatever reason, has turned into a lemon."

Donna was clearly confused and failed to comprehend the intricacies of what she had just been told.

"You know, Donna? A lemon! A sour citrus fruit. They normally grow on lemon trees although I once saw one grow underground like a radish."

"That can't be."

"It seems unbelievable, I know, but I swear, hand on heart, it was growing underground."

"No... I mean my heart. It can't be true it has become a lemon."

"Oh but I'm afraid it most certainly is. In the half hour you've been here we've run an implausible number of tests on you. The reality of the situation is confirmed beyond all reasonable doubt."

"But how does a perfectly human heart suddenly decide it wants to be a lemon? My mother! Could she have something to do with this?"

"You're mother?" Dr. Laurentis probed.

"Yes, my mother. You know…"

"You mean because your mother is a wedge of lemon?"

Donna nodded.

"I can understand how on the surface, your mother being a lemon wedge appears to be the most logical cause of your current situation. However, I feel it's important to state that there was nothing in the battery of tests we subjected you to that indicates a hereditary nature."

Dr. Laurentis had a dignified air of seriousness about him that chilled Donna to the pips. Vague hopes of this being some elaborate hoax were fading fast. There was nothing Donna could say that remotely articulated the complex stew of thoughts that simmered in her head. Instead she allowed her tears to flow freely. Dr. Laurentis immediately unzipped his pants and freed his throbbing erection. He looked at Donna shamefully and began to violently masturbate. Donna's look of abject horror convinced Dr. Laurentis that he really needed to offer explanation for his actions.

"I'm awfully sorry about this, Donna. Whenever I see a person crying, I must wank. Please don't tell my wife."

The room Susie awoke in was unusually bright, even to her newly opened eyes. After several minutes of reorientation it became apparent her arms were chained down to a wooden table and she wasn't going anywhere in a hurry.

"IAN!!!" she yelled over and over with elevating fear.

"You finally awake, Susie? I was beginning to think I'd have to wake you myself."

Ian now appeared on the table next to Susie, smiling at her

with unsympathetic eyes.

"What's happening, Ian? Why am I chained to the table?"

"You see Susie, as far as pomegranates go, I'm really not a very nice one. Essentially I've stolen you. Of course you *did* come willingly but I'd like to put that one down to the colorful little story I told you. Hell, if I had been you I would have taken me home too. Really, I can be quite convincing."

Susie began to weep in a way that would surely provoke the heart of any remotely decent person to irreparably break. Ian clearly wasn't one of those remotely decent people.

"How long have I been here? I have to get back to my mother. She must be so worried."

"Look, I can't say I have good news for you, Susie. Unless you believe in some wacky afterlife-type scenario you ain't ever going to see your mother again. From my perspective it's really quite a boon! Basically you're mine now, and I have a lot of model trains that need urgent assembly."

At those words Susie's tears completely stopped and an unnatural calm engulfed her. Her quivering lips morphed into a smile and the gentle sobbing turned into childish giggle.

"Oh, Ian," Susie beamed, "I do hope I can build these trains well for you."

"That's the spirit, Susie. Get into it!"

"When life gives you lemons, make lemonade." Those had been the rather hackneyed words Dr. Laurentis had used when discussing the possible solution to Donna's lemon heart. Donna had agreed to the procedure because she wasn't sure there was an alternative. She fondled the plastic tubing that jutted from her chest, feeling little spikes of pain where the incision had been made. To Donna, the solution seemed somewhat ill-conceived. The tubing wasn't subtle and would clearly become a topic of conversation for anyone who approached her. Dr. Laurentis had claimed her passing out was a result of the intense sourness Donna had felt immediately prior. He doubted such incidents would be life-threatening but posed his solution as a means of improving Donna's disposition and general quality of life. Dr. Laurentis theorized that the lemon Donna's heart had become was responsible for her sour attitude and the way to counteract such an occurrence was to apply a sweetening agent directly to the source of the sourness. The plastic tubing was inserted directly into the center of the lemon heart. Twice a day, Donna was to pour one teaspoon of white sugar into the tubing in a literal attempt to sweeten the lemon; hence altering her disposition into that of a more positive individual.

Donna's hand shook as she spooned the sugar down the tube, sincerely doubting that such a haphazard treatment could possibly work.

"This seems awfully strange to me," said the lemon wedge as she watched Donna closely. "Do you think it could possibly work?"

"You'll be in a better position to tell me that, mumsy bumsy." Donna's spite was uncontrollable.

The sugar crawled down the tube until it finally reached the lemon heart, and what a strange sensation it was. It was akin to burning but it wasn't necessarily painful. As a completely foreign experience however, it made Donna feel quite uncomfortable. She fell back into an armchair, listening to the strange puffing sounds coming from her chest. Her body had never felt so completely alien and it was a feeling that didn't sit well.

"Do you feel anything, Don?" asked the lemon wedge with a tremendous level of concern.

"I feel my bladder, mumsy. My bladder is informing me that piss is imminent and let me tell you, this piss is particularly interested in this very armchair."

"Please don't urinate on my armchair, Donna."

"No point pleading with me, mumsy." Donna parted her legs wide. "Talk to my bladder. I have no control."

She howled with childish laughter as the arc of urine soiled the armchair that the lemon wedge loved so much.

"I think it's safe to assume that the sugar hasn't had an effect yet."

"I think it's safe to assume that your assumption is fairly accurate, mumsy."

"Bloody hell, Susie. How many train sets did you say you'd built before?" asked Ian with genuine, awed surprise.

"I have never built a train set until today. Why?"

"Never? Well I'll be damned. You have enough dexterity in them fingers to unpick Egyptian cotton."

Susie giggled, slightly embarrassed yet strangely proud in the face of Ian's observation.

"Mother did mention my hands seemed somewhat clever. She says I shouldn't be able to assemble complicated machinery at my age. She tells me not to talk about it much because people may take advantage of me and have me finish their jigsaw puzzles and such."

"I can see where your mother's coming from. If I were your mother I don't imagine I'd be too eager to have my daughter assembling stranger's puzzles either. Now let me tell you something Susie."

"What's that, Ian?"

"I've decided I'm going to add three more carriages to this train."

"Three? That doesn't seem like very many."

"Well, I'm going to start you with three because that's all I currently have at hand. Does that make more sense?"

Susie giggled again, "Yes, Ian, that makes sense."

"I don't imagine it'll be simple, Susie. These extra carriages are ridiculous. I can't make heads nor tails of 'em. More parts than Rush's drum kit. I gotta say though, if you fuck it up, I may have to kill ya."

Susie spent some time writhing around in anxious excitement, the unbearable expectation weighing down upon her.

"This is going to be a fair amount of work isn't it, Ian?"

Ian let a gentle laugh escape his lips, unmistakably infused with fatherly nurture.

"Yes Susie, I do believe this will be pretty tiring for you."

Susie watched as Ian awkwardly nudged three rather large boxes toward her. The process took hours, but in Susie's excitement, it seemed mere seconds.

"Now then, Susie. Would you be so kind as to pick each box up in turn, remove the lids and pour out the multitude of contents in a dramatic fashion?

Susie had the boxes in her arms in an instant and poised herself to obey Ian's command.

"Now when ya do it, make out that it's not you doing it,

but me, and pretend for a moment, if you will, that you are somewhat overcome by it all. A little scared even."

Susie repressed her urge to giggle as she let the contents of the model train sets fall around her. She opened her mouth in a look of exaggerated surprise.

"Oh no! There is ever so many pieces. Whatever shall I do?"

Ian huffed. "You ain't about to win any Oscars, Susie, I can tell you that much. Didn't believe you were overcome for a second."

"I'm sorry… would you like me to do it again?"

"Nah, nah. Don't worry about it. I doubt you could do any better. Just get to building."

These new trains were definitely more convoluted than the previous ones Susie had assembled. She struggled to understand their logic and wondered if perhaps this might be some form of ruse.

"I just can't see how this is possible, Ian. There must be 5000 pieces here."

Ian appeared before her brandishing a switchblade in his impossible hand.

"Look… let's say you don't figure this out. My little glistening mate here is going to STAB you rather forcefully. Get it?"

Susie giggled. "Alright, Ian. I'll see what I can do."

"It's not working. She's worse, much, much worse."

The lemon wedge was shaking like a leaf, hiding in her bedroom closet with the phone pressed firmly against whatever she used to hear. Donna's rampage was drawing closer.

"You've got to give it time," Dr. Laurentis protested, trying to calm the situation.

"I really don't think I have much time left. She's drawn little cocks all over me. It's in permanent marker. It's not coming off any time soon."

"Have you tried calling the police?"

"Of course I've tried. They mentioned something about the shit stained hands of the town's aristocracy and said they were busy *watching something about a paper shortage*. He called me a sour bitch and hung up the phone. I really don't know what to do. You're my last resort, Dr. Laurentis."

"Shit, I don't know. Have you tried reasoning with her?"

The anger momentarily overrode any fear the lemon wedge had.

"Tried reasoning with her? She's pissing and shitting all over the place, Doctor. I really think we're well beyond the point of reason!"

As Dr. Laurentis hung up the phone in exasperation, Donna ripped the closet door off its hinges in a remarkable display of strength. The lemon wedge cowered pathetically, as close to the far corner of the closet as she could possibly get. It wasn't even close to far enough. Donna easily reached in and picked her up.

"I need a sting in my eye, mumsy."

"Put me down, Donna. You have no idea what you're doing!"

"I know what I'm doing. I just told you. I need a sting in my eye."

"What does that even mean?"

Donna answered the question via direct demonstration.

Holding her mother up above her face, Donna squeezed every ounce of life from the lemon wedge into her wide, greedy eyes. The horrific screaming turned into a gurgle as the lemon juice pooled in Donna's sockets before cascading down her cheeks like tears. Truth be told, the sting provoked a few real tears, which assimilated with the lemon juice before dripping from Donna's chin to the floor below.

"I got the eye sting, mumsy."

Donna was joyful yet sickened to her core. She held up the limp skin, pocked with rind and pulp. There was no escaping the reality that this spent flap of fruit was, or at least used to be, Donna's mother. Whether she liked it or not, Donna couldn't escape the implausible image of her birth. It had reached a point, no matter how fleeting, where the sickened part of Donna overrode the joy and she felt a desire for punishment. However relevant the concept of justice was, Donna desperately needed to feel herself crushed within the wheels of a just system. She mentally rehearsed her guilty plea in earnest before picking up the very same phone to talk to the very same police that had only moments ago hung up on her mother. Logically doubting the possibility they could have reached her mother in time, Donna still felt as if these so-called upholders of the law had ultimately handed her mother's death sentence out on a plate. Donna craved her own death sentence.

"Hello, police. I've killed my mother," Donna was quietly weeping.

"You've what?"

The police clearly heard but it wasn't often such a brazen admission crossed their path. Especially in such a small town where petty vandalism was usually the most serious offense dealt with on any given day.

"I've killed my mother." Donna repeated these words calmly, suppressing the weeping in order to aid her confession.

"You've killed your mother?"

Awkward silence ensued for several elongated seconds.

"How exactly did you kill your mother?"

"I squeezed her into my eye. I still have a touch of the eye sting."

"You what? Who is this?"

"It's Donna. Miss Donna Wedge from the old Miller estate."

"Donna Wedge? You're mother's a piece of lemon isn't she?"

Disbelief was clearly evident in the police officer's voice.

"Yes, sir. My mother was a wedge of lemon. Now she's just skin and pulp. I killed her. I deliberately squeezed the life out of her."

Laughter filled the line at the policeman's end. It was a chorus of laughter. It was evident that she was on speakerphone and confessing to an audience.

"What's so funny?"

"You silly twat! You can't be charged for killing a piece of fruit."

The policeman hung up the phone abruptly and Donna found herself talking with the cold, completely indifferent dial tone. She listened for some time before eventually putting the phone down and lying on the floor.

It was a real shame Susie hadn't been able to correctly assemble those model trains. She definitely tried her hardest, Ian was willing to concede at least that, but her hardest fell short of the mark. It was a model 822 Amtrak that did her in. From a casual distance it looked quite good, but closer inspection revealed slanted positioning of the decals. Such a misstep really upset the overall gravitas of the piece. There was even a pang of guilt when he first edged the switchblade into her stomach. She was definitely a trooper about it though. Ian smiled as he remembered the way she giggled as he drove the blade deeper.

"You tried, Susie, but you fucked up, didn't ya?"

"I'm so sorry, Ian. I really did make a bit of a mess of it."

"I'm gonna have to kill you a bit. It's just... I have to. You understand."

"Of course I do. You need to do what's right."

"Sorry I gotta do this. I liked ya."

"Never be sorry, Ian."

Donna had stopped feeling guilt over her mother's murder rather shortly after the event. The death of her mother was widely known throughout the town but nobody seemed to miss her too much, despite an initial outward attempt to act emotionally appropriate directly after the event. The townspeople took Donna's rapid acceptance as an invite to move on with their own lives, which they did very easily.

Susie's mother was found dead exactly two weeks after her daughter's abduction. As is typical in corpse discovery it was the smell that attracted the attention of a neighbor who saw fit to instantly notify the police when no amount of knocking upon the door yielded results. The death of a gravely ill individual is never much of a surprise but Susie's absence certainly was. There was a mild panic, which arose throughout the town as an elaborate search operation began. The search was largely spurred on by guilt. Susie was much loved around town and her absence should have been noted much earlier. Almost every door was knocked on, as the hunt for information intensified. I say 'almost every door' because nobody felt the need to confront Ian. People never suspect a pomegranate.

Donna was sitting in the only park in town by the pond. She was feeding ducks stale bread and staring pensively at nothing. Ian often rolled by the park to watch children, but on this particular day it was Donna who attracted his attention. Not being shy he felt completely comfortable approaching her and sitting right down on the bench next to her.

"You're Donna right?"

Everybody knew everybody in this town by marginal degrees of separation and news of the death of Donna's mother was widely circulated. Donna slowly turned her head to face Ian.

"Yes… I'm Donna. You're Ian, aren't you? I don't believe we've ever had the pleasure of conversation."

Ian smiled to himself and began a rocking motion, which approximated nodding.

"Yep, I'm Ian alright and the pleasure is all mine, let me assure you. I heard about your mother. That's tough news. We fruits have an affinity, I guess you could say."

Donna was silent for some time before eventually saying, "I'm a terrible person, Ian, a truly terrible person."

Ian was taken aback and was compelled to dredge up the source of Donna's current emotional state.

"What on earth are you talking about, girl? Don't try and tell me you're a terrible person without providing proof. Let me judge the merits of your little assertion."

"My mother Ian… I killed her. I picked her up in my hand and deliberately squeezed all of the juice right out of her. I squeezed her into my eye for reasons I can't quite understand."

Ian stared hard at Donna, searching for the right words.

"You weren't caught? Nobody questioned you?"

"That's the thing. I tried to get myself caught. I called the police immediately afterward. I still had the eye sting. They fucking laughed at me! Told me no one gets in trouble for killing a piece of fruit."

"You feel guilty?" Ian's tone was serious but filled with compassion.

"I feel guilty but not for the reason you'd expect. I feel guilty because I don't feel guilty if that makes any sense. It's like a multi-level guilt complex. You see I'm no longer upset about mother's death. It doesn't affect me in the slightest and this makes me feel guilty because I know it *should* affect me. It's all screwy."

Once again Ian rock-nodded. "I think I understand what you're saying."

Donna stared hard at Ian searching for truth in his understanding. She believed she found it and felt a great deal of comfort at this thought. Once more silence ensued for some time. Ian eventually broke this silence simply by saying, "Perhaps you're just a bad person."

Rather than getting defensive, Donna nodded in agreement.

"You know, Ian... I think you may be right. I don't know what to do about it though. Can I tell you something?"

"Of course you can, Donna. Go for it."

"My heart... It's turned into a lemon. That's gotta have something to do with it."

She prodded the tube jutting from her chest.

"Why? Because lemons are sour?"

"I guess, yeah."

"Nonsense! Your mother... She was a lemon, was she not?"

"A wedge of lemon, yes."

"Was she what you'd call a *bad* person?"

"I guess not."

"Exactly! Your mother was one of those hopelessly nice people. She was nice to the core. I wouldn't say there was an ounce of bad in her at all. Now, can I tell you something?"

Donna nodded.

"Me, I'm a pomegranate. Comparatively I'm a rather sweet fruit. A little tart perhaps but compared to a lemon I'm pretty fucking sweet. Now, despite all of this sweet I have bubbling inside me I'm an absolutely wretched person. A real nasty piece of work."

"How so?"

"I steal children and get 'em to build trains for me. If they can't do it, I kill 'em. You remember Susie?"

"Of course. She went missing. What? You killed her?" Donna was enthralled.

"You bet your arse I did."

Donna muttered some profanity under her breath that Ian couldn't quite make out.

"You don't know what to say do you? The point is we are

who we are despite *what* we are. We're both absolute nasty cunts and if there's a hell we're going there. No doubt about it."

Donna was silent but Ian's words were easy for her to accept.

"I think you're right, Ian."

"Of course I'm right. I've spent a lot of time thinking about this kinda stuff. I've reached the stage where I know what the hell I'm on about."

Donna was still silent.

"Look, Donna… I think you need some rest. It can be a bit hard when forced to accept the fact you're a bad person. Don't worry though. You'll come to love it."

"Once again, I think you're right, Ian."

Donna slowly stood up and walked away, leaving Ian sitting on the bench. Donna tugged at the tube in her chest, resolving never to force sugar into her heart again.

FLIP TO SIDE A TO CONTINUE READING

MICHAEL J SEIDLINGER'S

MESSES OF MEN

LAZY FASCIST DOUBLE #1

ALSO BY MICHAEL J SEIDLINGER

The Face of Any Other

The Fun We've Had

The Laughter of Strangers

Mother of a Machine Gun

The Strangest

MESSES OF MEN

Michael J Seidlinger

LAZY FASCIST PRESS

LAZY FASCIST PRESS
PO Box 10065
Portland, OR 97296

www.lazyfascistpress.com

ISBN: 978-1-62105-179-4

Printed in the USA.

1.

The taxicab sat purring idly. Right side hugged the curb. Taxicabs cluttered the city's streets turning the evening on to a familiar yellow glow. The yellow fluid of the city coursed through its streets. Inside the Driver waited for the Customer. The Driver sat rigid watching the other cabs enviously. They were cabs with somewhere to go. The Driver kept one hand on the wheel and the other hand feeling the underside of the dashboard where a 9mm handgun was hidden, held up by five strips of duct tape. The Driver called it Safety while anyone else could only call it an easy escape. The Driver was anxious but ready. He looked up at the top floors of the four-star hotel. Lights flickered on and off.

The lobby doors slid open and closed automatically. Shapes moving. They are people coming and going. They are people on the rise and people on the fall.

Any one of these people could be the Customer.

Any one of these people could give the Driver somewhere to go. Giving the taxicab a destination meant giving the Driver some greater purpose by providing public service. Public service pays in cash and leaves a big tip.

Most shapes are clustered into twos, threes, groups leaving the lobby of the hotel. Very few people dare to be seen alone in this city.

People leave, and occasionally there's a single shape.

Single shapes are easy fares. The Driver pulled the car into drive leaving his foot on the brakes.

This should be the Customer. Where to, the Driver will ask when the shape turns into one of those people. The Customer will sit down in the back seat. Busy a moment with his things the Customer will look up at the Driver who's staring intently at the Customer through the rearview mirror.

The Customer will provide a destination and the Driver will be off. Meter ticking away. Each dollar a donation to the Driver.

The Customer will provide and the Driver will take him there.

The meter ticked away. The Driver put the taxicab back into park. Released the brakes. He tapped the meter.

Anywhere. I will take you. Anywhere. We must go.

The Customer was slumped in the backseat.

Hey. The Driver doesn't call people sir. Hey you. Let's go!

Go?

Yes. Yes. Where to? Meter's ticking.

I have nowhere to go.

Anywhere. I can take you.

I don't have anywhere to go.

Why you in my cab?

I want to go somewhere where I can't go back.

I can. I can take you. Expensive, but I can take you. Tapping the top of the meter, And expensive. Very.

I don't want to go anywhere.

Where to, friend? The Driver started to pressure the Customer. The Customer wasn't playing Customer right.

I don't want to go anywhere. I don't have anywhere to go. I want to stay right here. Right now. This moment. And night.

I don't want anything to change. Everything that's changed has turned against me.

No more changing. No more. I can't.

Where to?

I have nowhere to go. Don't you understand?

You are now $2.86 and going nowhere.

I have nowhere else to go.

Then why not off yourself? It's easier. The Driver tapped the meter yet again, And cheaper. Much much cheaper. I can find you a price. Real cheap. Talking good pistol. Name brand. I can take you to as you say where you no go back. I have a friend. He can take you there. We go. Okay?

No. Suicide? What's that going to do?

You have nowhere to go. You say buh-byes. You say no-more. It's better that way. Not alone, friend. Not at all. Lots of people lying down the last time.

No.

We must go. Anywhere. But we must go.

The Customer reached into his pocket and pulled out his wallet. If money is such a fucking problem. He pulled out a wad of bills. Mixture of twenties, fifties, and quite a few hundred-dollar-bills. Take it. Friend. Stop saying we need to go. I just need to think. Take it.

Sure. Sure. The Driver turned off the meter and counted the cash.

The Customer sat idly while the Driver counted. He did not look out the window at the people and yellow cabs fluttering by. He sat there as if the backseat was separate from the world on the other side of that car door.

The Driver slapped the stack and stowed it away out of view. We can wait here. It is up to you. But I can take you.

Anywhere. Anywhere and we will go. For the price I can take you as far as you will need. What you need. We all need. I can take you to what you need.

The Customer frowned.

I can. I can. I can take you. I am here. We can talk too. Like now. You say something. I say something. We will talk. Anything and we can talk.

2.

He was leaving the hotel and leaving what had already passed him by. It was a business venture but not only that. It was also a significant other. It was also a family that had seemingly died off one by one while he was too ignorant and selfish living in this city to give them a call and keep in touch.

It was also that significant other saying it was over.

That significant other stayed behind in the hotel.

That significant other now owned half of all his things. That significant other now owned half of his business.

And that business. He had seen its initial breakthrough into its soul-crushing defeat. But like him it still floated. It still existed but just barely.

That significant other owned half of what was already owned by the banks and his other investors. Sixty six percent. Maybe seventy. It wasn't his anymore.

And now that significant other wanted half of what he still had.

Sure. Why not.

He lost that too. He had no place to live. They had lived together. They never had kids. He never did anything with

himself but work. Continue to work.

It's easy to stomach what comes at you daily.

Everyone toyed with the fantasy of never making it to morning.

This night he simply had nowhere else.

Nowhere to go. No reason to. No purpose. No feeling. No desires to be anywhere. No one to meet. No needs.

It's quite simply a mess.

In the thick of the mess he is nothing. He feels nothing. He simply wants everything to stop. And contrary to the driver's assumptions that doesn't mean suicide. Suicide is too glamorous. Too much of a personal statement.

There is nothing personal about this.

He wants everything to stop. Hit the stop button on the city.

Let him just sit there calmly and let him sit. He simply wants to sit.

To be idle.

To think. Probably not.

He is at his last.

The last of his funds and that means every dollar to his name or otherwise the extent of his worth he just gave to the driver. The driver counted his worth in under two minutes. He can't be worth that much then.

Well then, there really isn't much of anything left for the Customer. He truly has nowhere to go. If anything, he wants to stay right here. He wants to sit idly growing hungry and weak.

He wants the night and to stay with the night.

And perhaps he now wants the damn driver to shut the hell up.

He is a mess.

3.

The Driver was taking him somewhere. The Customer didn't want to go. I take you. I take you. You'll like very much.

Somehow he was certain he wouldn't.

The city looked the same.

In daylight and in the dark of night it looked exactly the same.

Every street was full of shapes moving. Searching.

The streets were clogged with these taxicabs.

Nobody could afford cars anymore.

The alleys were full of trash living and dead. Lately there have been more dead than the living.

The windows of buildings all remained unlit.

So much for the concrete jungle twinkling. A lot of people boarded up their windows. Just enough to create their own little sanctuaries inside their small cramped apartments.

We go. See.

The Customer didn't look out the window. By the distance and how long it took and left or right which turns the driver took he knew precisely where the damn driver took him.

Yeah. That club. The club he had been to once. Twice.

We go. You drink little or a lot. I take you so you are okay.

The Customer was already buzzed. He had been drinking for twenty years. A few more drinks would do nothing but remind him of how poor he really was. He couldn't afford to pay for even the one drink.

His body couldn't stand another drink.

Sickness is a few sips away.

The Driver pulled into a parking space in the back of the

club. The taxicab turned off. They both sat in darkness.

The Driver stared patiently at the Customer through his rearview mirror. The Customer didn't move, didn't leave the backseat. He sat there.

Idle.

We go. Come.

The Driver opened his door and stepped out of the taxicab.

The Customer didn't sigh. He didn't frown. He didn't feel anything. Not disappointment. Not irritation or anger. Surely he did not want to go inside the club but he also didn't feel like he didn't want to go inside the club.

He just sat there until the Driver was at his door opening it.

The Customer stepped out.

They went inside.

4.

The club and every other club on any night in the city is overflowing with people that want to turn back into shapes. They go there to socialize. They go there to disappear. They want to confuse their identities into thinking they are someone else. Better yet, nobody.

The Customer walked over to the bar. Somewhere between stepping inside the loud club and making the six or seven steps to the bar he misplaced the Driver. The Driver was no longer at his side.

No bother.

At the bar he didn't order a drink. He stood there and when a seat opened up he moved through the crowd. The bartender zoned in on him and asked him what he wanted to

drink. He went for water, playing the typical drunk so that the bartender wouldn't ask if he was a deadbeat or not.

Shapes filtered all around.

Shapes turned into arms reaching for refills and new drinks. They seemed to drink more than pay for their drinks.

Someone tapped him on the shoulder.

He looked back but there was nobody there.

Almost immediately it happened again. A tap.

Nobody.

He returned to his water.

Something caught his eye. He looked at the far end of the bar. Someone was staring at him and making no effort to hide the fact that they were staring at him.

He returned to his water.

He looked over. Someone still stared.

The Customer got up and left the bar with his water and wandered the club. He avoided the dance floor where people didn't really dance. They dry humped and stumbled around like zombies. Every once in a while one of them tripped and fell. Everyone else came falling too. Like dominoes.

He sipped his water.

He sat down in a booth somewhere in the back where the music wasn't as loud and didn't notice that someone was already sitting there.

Another man with a line of empty glasses and a smile so fake it might be tattooed onto his face.

Hey.

The Customer said Hey.

Hey.

Hey.

How many do you have in you?

The Customer thought about this for a second. Drinks. Right. How many drinks. He lied. Ten.

I feel ya.

The Customer crunched on a piece of ice.

What time is it?

I don't know.

Okay.

Are you?

Huh?

Okay. Are you okay?

The man counted the empty glasses. The Customer counted along with him. With the glasses they could reach the number twenty-nine.

Twenty-nine. That's a lot to drink.

Somehow not enough. I'll tell you, this music is what's going to push me over the edge.

Yeah. The music is pretty bad.

Bad? It's a bunch of razorblades in a washing machine.

Okay.

The man downed the rest of his thirtieth drink. A waitress manifested from thin air and gave him another.

So. What do you do?

The Customer parried, What do you do?

The man had trouble putting it into words. He gave up. He shrugged. He looked at his suit which was damp, probably a mixture of spilt liquor and sweat. Yeah. It is kind of hot in here.

The music.

Come on. Let's get out of here.

The Customer followed.

They ended up back in the parking lot behind the club.

He followed the man up and down the six aisles of cars once. Twice. Three times. Maybe five. Until the man found his car.

He took out his keys. He tried to unlock the car.

It wasn't his.

They searched around a while longer.

They came to a black sports car. Pretty impressive.

The Customer said, You own a car.

The man stumbled and propped himself up on the car. Yeah. Everybody does. The man motioned to the parking lot. It was true. The lot was full of vehicles that weren't taxicabs.

The man said, What do I do. It wasn't a question. What do I do. I do enough to have this car. Have a wife. A house. Kids. I think I have three now. Not sure. Lemme check. The man searched his pockets for an expensive looking wallet.

My car. The man pointed to the car. The Customer remembered.

Yes. That is your car. It is a nice car.

It is isn't it.

The man said, This is my wife. The man held out a picture. It was a magazine clipping of some model. It wasn't even clipped. It was torn out haphazardly and the image was wrinkled and faded.

She is pretty.

The man nodded. Beautiful. Just beautiful. I do it all for her…

This is my house.

The man held out a document. The Customer couldn't read it in the dark parking lot but the bold red stamp was obvious enough. Foreclosure.

It is a beautiful house.

It is isn't it.

The man reached into a back pocket and took something else out.

These are my kids. His kids looked like death threats from someone named Cindy. The death threats indicated the man's name was Jeff.

Jeff had his eyes closed.

They are beautiful kids. The Customer looked down at the license plate of the car. It had one of those temporary paper tags. Faded and torn.

The date on the tag was expired.

The man named Jeff said, What do you do?

He replied, What do you do?

The man named Jeff said, On the shitter I don't piss or shit. I cry. I sob like a school girl. I walk out of there with eyes glowing pure. I leave fear in the shitter unflushed.

Isn't that what a shitter is for. You get rid of the shit. All kinds of shit.

The man named Jeff agreed. Hell yes. We have to deal with all kinds of shit. There isn't just the one and the two. There's the twenty and the twelve. And that's already passed. Not the year. The number twenty. The number twelve.

How much shit do you have to deal with.

Enough to count to fifty.

What do you do? The man named Jeff asked the Customer yet again.

This time the Customer answered. I am a businessman.

The man named Jeff coughed. He kept coughing. No. No. Not what you do. I am asking what do you do!

What do you do.

What do I do?

The Customer replied, Well what do you do?

I have this car see and I have these drinks in me right.

Oh come on.

I also have this lighter. And I have this bottle of bleach.

The Customer listened.

I also have this bucket and this partially eaten fast food cheeseburger.

Yeah?

That's what I'm going to do.

What are you going to do?

A yellow cab pulled up. The man named Jeff stopped talking, interrupted by the cab. The Driver sat there. The Driver waved.

He was waving at the Customer.

The man named Jeff asked, Do you think he's real?

The Customer replied, I don't know.

The man named Jeff immediately went back to talking about whatever he was going to do. I have this space I need to fill. See. I have all these things. I can fill the space. I filled it once. I can fill it again.

Why do you need to fill it?

You need to have a space of your own.

Do you?

The man named Jeff opened his mouth to speak then closed it. His head bobbled ever so slightly. The Customer noticed.

That's a lot of space to fill. Do you think you'll ever fill it?

The man named Jeff replied, Yeah.

Do you ever think you'll be satisfied enough?

Yeah.

Why such a big space?

The man named Jeff stared at the side of the taxicab. Everyone's got to have a home to crawl back to every night.

Where are you staying?

The man named Jeff said nothing more. He looked at his car and tried getting into the driver's seat but failed. He hit his head on the top of the car shouting nonexistent profanities and then failing to sit down he decided to splay himself out across the driver and front passenger seats.

The Customer watched as the man named Jeff kicked the car door closed.

Back inside the taxicab the Driver was talking.

I find you and I take care of you. See. I take care of you. Remember car. Number 6. 6. Okay. Number 6. What you need. Number 6.

The Driver started down a random street. He didn't ask the Customer Where to. This time the Customer provided a destination.

It was what he said.

He said, I don't want to go forward. I don't want to go back.

I don't want tomorrow to come.

I want tonight. I want to stay with the night.

All the while the Driver was nodding as if in agreement. As if he understood. I take. I take you. Yes.

The Customer had his eyes closed. His head craned back.

The Driver sped forward, a destination in mind.

5.

The night is young. That's what the Driver said to the

Customer but the Customer wasn't listening. The Customer was quiet and lifeless in the backseat.

He wasn't sleeping. He was doing his best impression of the deceased.

When the Customer opened his eyes the taxicab was parked at a gas-pump. The Driver was outside the cab filling the tank. The Customer sat up in his seat.

He thought about it.

Decided against it.

He went inside the quick-stop instead. There were all kinds of artery-clogging snacks there.

Shapes pulled themselves apart from the night to enter the blinding light of these quick-stops to buy their weight in shit so that later they may feel like shit.

And be reminded of what a mess this really can be.

The Driver waited at the gas pump.

All was ready to go.

Food. Good. You must eat.

The Customer said, I don't see a clock in this cab.

No. No. There is clock. See. See. The Customer couldn't see a clock.

After the third bite of his donut he didn't care. He didn't care about the taste either. It was all about the texture. The swallow. The feeling of being full.

The sensation of doing something.

The Driver started off towards some part of the city.

The Customer couldn't be bothered.

6.

There was another taxicab following them. The Customer saw

it first. It was the Driver that mentioned it. She with you?

How do you know it's a she?

No. No. I don't know. Maybe a he. Maybe a she.

The Customer looked out the back of the taxicab as the Driver maintained his speed. No need to speed.

Not a chase. Not a chase.

The Customer said, Not yet.

He watched as the tail switched lanes whenever the Driver switched lanes. When they stopped at a red light the Driver strategically maneuvered the taxicab like a snake to the far right. When they made a right the tail kept with them.

The Customer lost interest.

We go faster? Problem? No. Yes. No?

No.

The Driver drove. The Customer sat.

Where are we going? was what he said before he even knew he was saying it.

The Driver was talking again assuring him he was taking him to his destination. Sit. Sit. Enjoy this ride. I take. I take you. No problem.

They didn't manage to lose the tail.

7.

Their trail was like a red line across the city. You could figure out where they started and where they stopped but all the distractions, shortcuts and extraneous moments were left a part of the ceaseless yellow blur of the night.

The night glowed. Certainly it was getting later.

What time is it.

The Driver said it was early. Much to do. We go. The Driver pointed his finger towards their right. They had made it to another part of the city.

The Customer had been here only once before. When he used to take the subway he frequently missed his stop and would end up in the nether-regions of the city. He was the type to stay in the center. Downtown. The failing heart.

This place was north of the downtown area.

The shapes here were stagnant. Nothing moved.

Bouncers walked the streets like ghosts.

There was one on every street corner around here.

The Driver waved to one. The bouncer lifted his chin once.

At least they lost the tail.

The Customer reasoned that this was why the driver brought him here.

But they didn't leave.

The Driver circled a few blocks making one right turn after the next.

The Customer sat idle and unconvinced.

What?

Oh nothing.

8.

The yellow streak didn't reach this part of the city. They were the lone taxicab here. Nobody drives down these streets.

The streets were drained and yet still dripping wet. Puddles as if it just recently rained. There was only one other vehicle on the road. A truck decked out. It couldn't be street-legal. It tore up a four-way intersection.

Nobody seemed to notice.

The Driver pulled the taxicab into a space in front of a building lit up with a pale white florescence. This was odd for this part of the city.

So what.

Yes?

Problem friend?

The Customer said, No.

The truck spun in circles and crashed into nearby storefronts.

No reason to stop. Soon the truck would stop on its own.

The truck nearly hit a bouncer. The bouncer didn't move.

Got to keep up that image of confidence and safety.

9.

The Driver turned the ignition and got out of the taxicab. The Customer followed because the driver wanted to make sure the taxicab wouldn't be stolen.

Come. Come. I need to lock it.

Everybody and everything needs to be safe even if it isn't logical.

Even if it doesn't feel right.

The Customer looked at the driver who then wandered inside the illuminated building. He looked up at the marquee.

Yeah. No wonder. They sell things. Not just anything too. The kind of stuff people drive to these parts of the city to buy because it's cheaper, it's better quality.

These things keep you safe. So safe you don't even remember what it feels like to be in danger. You are safe but afraid.

These things should come with a word-of-warning. He made sure everything that was his would be safe and all it did was make him even more concerned about their safety. Was it working. Was it working right.

The Customer walked towards the man. The man said, Hello. Please, have a seat.

The Customer sat next to him. My name is Andrew.

Andrew didn't ask for the Customer's name.

As you might have guessed that is my truck. Yes. But I have my reasons. They can't find me if the trail ends right here.

The Customer replied, Who?

Excuse me? Anyway I am twenty-nine years old. I am still young. I have a great job and a lot of great stuff. I have a wife and I have a life.

Great life.

I see, said the Customer.

I have to keep things safe.

Yeah. You do.

Yes. I do. I need to make sure nothing is stolen. Especially my identity.

Yeah. You don't want anyone else to be you.

Andrew's left leg was soaked through with blood.

I can walk. Don't worry about that.

Okay. I won't worry.

I can't let them find me. I make sure I'm safe but then they still manage to find me.

The bouncer from the opposite streetcorner walked up to them. The Customer watched Andrew watching the bouncer get closer. He watched as Andrew grew noticeably more concerned the closer the bouncer got.

His hands were shaking.

When the bouncer reached them Andrew cried out, You can't take me!

The bouncer didn't seem to hear Andrew and instead said, You can't sit in the middle of the road. It isn't safe.

The Customer stood up. The bouncer grabbed at Andrew and pulling him up to his feet. Can you walk?

Yes. I can.

Alright. The bouncer looked around. The truck ain't going nowhere. You'll have to take a cab. There's one. The bouncer pointed to the parked taxicab. The number two. Take it. Go home. Stop chasing shit that won't ever change.

The Driver was seated behind the wheel.

The Customer got into the backseat. Andrew followed.

The Driver turned back onto the street.

Oh. Andrew perked up. There's a great restaurant down this road somewhere.

Everything tastes bad.

Are you kidding? That's a joke. Must be. Food's maybe the only thing worth living for. The city has some of the best restaurants in the country.

The Driver remained quiet.

Andrew did all the talking. Really. It's amazing food. Some of the best burgers I've ever tasted.

The Customer said, An amazing place in this neighborhood.

Hard to believe, huh? Yes. They make sure it's kept safe though. Just like me. They can't find me now. The truck won't lead back to me. Everybody I care about, they won't be able to find. Nope. Everything will be okay. It'll be alright. Perfectly fine. Yes. But seriously we need to go to this restaurant

The Driver replied, I take you. We go.

Andrew glanced up at the Driver.

He isn't real is he?

The Customer numbly replied, I don't know.

It isn't safe if I'm not driving.

We need to stop here. Right here. Stop the cab!

The Driver pulled up to what appeared to be an empty block. The entire block completely vacated. For Lease signs plastered everywhere. More than a few windows boarded up.

Andrew ran out of the taxicab.

The Customer ran after. He shouted, Where are you going?

Andrew bellowed, It's there! There! Just a few blocks away. Great food. Really really amazing food. Andrew stopped running.

He turned around and asked the Customer, How will we pay for the food?

With money.

I don't have money. I only have credit cards and they don't work anymore.

Work? So you're tapped out then.

Andrew chewed his nails. Yes. But I'm okay. Everything I hid away. No one can find her. No one can find me. Becca will stay beautiful.

Becca huh. The wife?

Yes. She is my wife. I made sure she's safe. I made sure of it. She wouldn't be able to find her way back even if she escaped. Do you have ID?

The Customer replied, Well yeah of course I have ID.

Andrew went pale. The depth of his voice disappeared leaving a shrill hollow voice that said, I need to go.

The Customer started to follow but Andrew told him to stop.

Having you around isn't safe. You'll only make a mess of things.

Seems to me things are already at that point.

I can't lose track of it. I can't. I tell myself to remain calm and keep track of everything. Always be safe and things will be alright. Things are too good, they're trying to find me so that they can make things go bad.

Andrew placed a hand over his mouth, You are one of them!

Andrew ran away from the Customer. The Customer turned around and returned to the taxicab.

The Driver said, He did not pay.

The Customer replied, He's had enough.

They continued driving. They did not pass by any so-called restaurant. The entire nine block stretch was abandoned. Nobody bothered with these areas anymore. They didn't even dump their garbage in such places.

The entire patch was so clean. The Customer looked at a digital marquee of yet another bank. Between phrases selling new incentives for starting a new checking account the marquee blinked in red the current time.

It must have been set wrong because it didn't seem that early.

The Driver said, We go.

I don't want to go anywhere.

We go. I take you.

I like it here.

Waste of time friend. Big waste of time. Much better. I take you.

10.

They passed by Andrew who was still running. When he saw

the taxicab he screamed and ran the other way. The Customer called out to Andrew.

Where are you going?

Andrew was screaming, Make it stop! Make it stop! Make it stop!

Make what stop?

The Driver said, No. No. No use. Don't talk to that man. He is sick.

He looked healthy enough to me.

No. No. He is sick.

Andrew disappeared into an alley out of sight.

He would never be seen again.

They kept driving. The Customer didn't feel sorry for him. He didn't feel much of anything. For a moment he toyed with the idea of that being him.

It's easy to get lost. Easy enough to disappear in an alley.

He dropped the idea almost immediately. Sure. It was easy. It just didn't seem like it would be the kind of idea that would stick.

So thought the guy who didn't have anywhere to go.

Nothing to behold. Nothing more to become.

This night is enough.

11.

I can't face tomorrow. Not that there's anything specific about tomorrow. It's yet another day with its many hurtful devices.

The very same devices that have been used before but I doubt if I still can.

If I still can walk talk drive and deliver the way I have in the past.

If, and that's always the question I don't want to answer.
I think what I could never say to anyone.
I feel more like a mess when I look my cleanest.
Pressed suit. New haircut. Sturdy handshake.
Glimmer of intent.
Don't see that now.

12.

Their faces turned to glare at him as the taxicab passed. Every single person on the street turned as if expecting to see something disgusting.

They all had the same faces.

They weren't wearing masks. They weren't doubles triples and quadruples of the same person. He wasn't asleep.

They watched him as if he were a dead man.

As if they expected to see him fall.

And someone was keeping track.

The traffic slowed the taxicab to a crawl. They entered the busiest streets of the city. The Customer had no clue where the Driver was taking him.

Someone walked with the cab. The one person that wasn't glaring at him. He walked as if keeping up with the taxicab.

That someone then took out a cellphone or a camera and took a picture of the taxicab. The Customer couldn't get a good look at the guy's face.

It was as if the guy didn't have a face.

Then he disappeared back into the shadows and shapes of people staring at the taxicab. Staring at the Customer.

Watching him.

They weren't though. They were staring through the taxicab window, through him and out to the other side of the street where something more important, something that interested the public, was happening.

A band played on some stage set up in an emptied parking lot.

The band played loud enough to be heard inside the taxicab.

The city intruded upon the relative safety of the taxicab's backseat.

The Customer did not like it.

The Driver killed the engine.

Hey...

We stop. They stop. We stop too.

They had closed the street. Blockades were set at the other end of the block. The drivers of other taxicabs reluctantly left their cabs for the show that had erupted into its first eardrum-punishing rage.

The Driver said, We go. We listen. Then we leave.

The Customer looked around for a clock. Found none.

We have time. We make time later.

The Customer replied, Yeah. Sure.

They both left the taxicab for the crowd gathered around the stage.

The Driver didn't bother locking the taxicab.

13.

The Driver did all the pushing while the Customer did all the following. Pushed deep into the crowd of people for reasons

that you could assume were to get a better look at the stage.

The music could be heard a number of blocks away so it wasn't just to get a better listen. It actually became more difficult to hear the music the closer they got. The Customer ducked and didn't bother looking at the bodies scraping by.

Touching skin.

Smelling of smoke and sweat.

The odor of people worrying into the night.

The Driver stopped and grabbed at the Customer. Look. Look. See. The music. And hesitating for a second the Driver looked at the band playing onstage. Beautiful? Beautiful music. Yes?

The Customer replied, Yes.

We listen. We enjoy.

The Customer couldn't say he enjoyed the music. It went on for a while.

14.

One song melded into the next. He could just feel time being wasted. The band wasn't nearly as interesting as everyone else made them out to be. The Customer started observing the crowd. This audience all had the very same face.

Faces blank and intently hopeful.

Necks bent in an almost painful way at the gods on the stage.

Gods only because they were able to muster up the courage to get up on the stage and play music that wasn't copied from somewhere else. Gods raised ever-so-slightly above them if only because at one point in their lives these musicians might

have been forced to live in the alleys of the city.

He misplaced the Driver. No register of surprise.

He was close enough to the stage to have the music be one abrasive mesh. It was far easier when you couldn't make out anything specific. The path to the nonexistent backstage was only a barricade climb away.

The bouncers looked exactly the same.

The Customer signaled to be picked out of the crowd.

A bouncer shuffled forward and picked him up by the neck as if he were a liquor bottle.

On the other side of the barricade it looked like everyone had lent out their eyes.

A congregation of whatevers.

The Customer took to the path leading back around to the street. At a fork the path offered access to the maybe nonexistent backstage. He took that right seeing that the street would be no different than the area around the stage.

The path narrowed until he had to walk sideways, squeezing between luggage and assorted machinery and crates.

Eventually he came to an opening.

This open area was filled with people that didn't seem to want to look him straight in the eye.

Experts of evasion every single person there were utilizing master-level strategies so that it didn't seem like they were trying to avoid other peoples' glares. But they were.

It was always a matter of picking something up or signing something or glancing off into the distance artistically or busying themselves with some conversation with others that also managed to appear nonchalant while never falling face-to-face.

He watched and listened.

He too avoided eye contact. The Customer went to catering.

Free food tasted the same. It tasted like ash.

He ate it anyway.

The crowd was cheering.

Maybe the show was ending.

15.

Turns out the show was only starting to pick up. The band had played the same song enough times that now nobody could tell the difference.

So they played the song again.

The Customer found a seat and sat there staring at the ground.

Someone dropped a book bag inches from the Customer's feet and sat down next to him. This man didn't have a problem making eye contact.

The man was young. And yet there were wrinkles forming under his eyes.

Soon they'd look like they were floating in two hollowed out sockets.

The Customer recognized this man.

He said, Why would you take a picture of someone like me?

The young man said, Hell you talking about? Never seen you before and I remember every face. Got to because they keep changing.

And a sigh. Something muffled and then another sigh.

The man was tired.

Too young to be tired.

Well I am, replied the young man.

Okay.

You don't understand.

Of course I do.

No you don't.

Maybe I don't.

You see… it used to make sense. I had a specific need. All I needed was myself to figure it out. I figured it out. Did it myself. DIY. All on my own.

Mr. DIY picked up the book bag and zipped it open. He opened it up wide enough so that the Customer could have a look. Various cans and rolls of paper or stickers or what-have-you crammed into the bag. Faint stench of vinegar. Definitely some kind of chemical.

I needed this. The danger. The danger defined why I did it and why I needed it. Now everybody needs what I have been doing for such a long time. I don't need their money. I don't need their love for what I do.

Mr. DIY trailed off.

Perhaps the Customer was supposed to say something. He didn't say anything.

Mr. DIY continued, I got what I needed. What appeared to be what I need. Now I need something else. But I can't leave this. It follows me. Their faces change before I can capture them. Before I can take a fucking picture. And before I finish one I've got five more.

I can't keep posting these. It defeats the purpose.

I only need myself. Now I can't do anything by myself. I have to wait until I get a call. They tell me where to post the pictures. Where to paint the adverts. I used to represent free

expression. Now I represent free enterprise.

I have like a hundred grand on me in cash. I don't need the money.

I needed the mission. Now my missions pay well but do nothing. They mean nothing. I don't need this. I thought I needed it but I don't need this.

It's no longer a game.

It is no longer me.

What do I need?

What exactly are you going to do?

I got a call. I have the posters. I climb up a couple stories. Glue them. Maybe I'll fall down. Maybe I'll break a leg. Maybe both.

I'll sit in the hospital. I'll be a victim and a hero. I don't need them to tell me what I am. I used to do this all by myself and for myself.

That's all I need.

I need it back the way it was.

However I can clean this up I need to make things simpler.

The Customer sat there listening. He wasn't much of a confidant.

Eventually Mr. DIY stood back up. Looked at his wristwatch. He said, I have to get this over with.

The Customer asked him what time it was.

Mr. DIY said, It's time to get this over with.

16.

Later the Customer was still sitting by himself in what he assumed was the backstage. It wasn't the backstage. Another

man asked for ID.

The Customer fumbled around for his license.

Not this. I need to see a guest pass. Not a license.

Guest pass.

The man seemed more than a little upset.

The Customer said, I'm sorry.

You shouldn't encourage him.

Who do I have to encourage?

He's still battling the reality of his success. As his agent I feel obligated to follow him to make sure he doesn't try something too risky. He is too valuable to see him get hurt or flame-out. He has a future in this business.

Yeah he does have a future.

Don't patronize me. He really does. He changed the way we advertise music all with the power of the message.

I haven't gotten the message.

The man cursed. Oh please! There's no message to get. Are you this fucking dense? I'm talking metaphorically. The message as in the client. The message as in doing the job the right way. The message as in getting fucking paid. The message as in playing up some critical and dangerous mission or whatever he calls it just to keep him stable.

Nobody is stable. Everybody is borderline schizophrenic.

That might be. All the more reason that everybody ought to have someone looking out for them.

I am my own man. Whatever that might mean.

The man gestured with eyes, Are you so sure?

The Customer turned and saw the Driver. The Driver was already talking.

We go. We go. I take you. We must. Music is over. We must go.

The Customer turned back to the man. The man said,

Everybody has someone looking out for them.

The Customer stood up from the chair. Stretched his legs and started off towards the Driver.

Before leaving the man whispered into the Customer's ear, He isn't real is he?

The Customer said numbly, I don't know.

17.

They got into the taxicab which had the number 4 plastered on its side. The Customer asked the Driver if they were in the right cab.

They all looked the same.

It was difficult for him to tell them apart.

The Driver assured him it was his taxicab.

My taxi. Yes. I keep it clean. Can only be mine.

The Customer hesitated.

Friend. No problem. See.

No problem.

Yes. Yes. No problem.

It was eerie but convenient that the place cleared up so quickly. By the time they got back to the taxicab everybody in front of them had cleared out.

Those waiting for them honked violently on their horns.

And they were off but they only made it a few blocks.

It only took a few blocks for the confusion to reach the Customer.

18.

Maybe it wasn't right to call it confusion. The Customer wasn't confused. But the word could be taken for one of its lesser meanings. Confusion as in there had been a mishap and the taxicab and the Customer had been involved.

Of course they weren't told beforehand that they would be involved.

Mr. DIY had looked quite similar to the Customer before he fell. Before he finished whatever he had planned.

It wasn't fatal but it was firmly against the law.

Despite what Mr. DIY had talked about, his actions were never all his own. They had a paper trail. They reached out far enough to include the Customer.

The Driver tried to stop the two cops from taking the Customer.

No. He is not the one. He is not the one.

The Driver repeated a number of times. Maybe he believed that if he said it enough times it would stick. It would be treated as valid testimony.

Sir. Come with us.

The Customer's aimless gaze spun in circles around the city that seemed all of a sudden like it was close. Too close. Suffocating. His eyes landed on a clock a block away. He couldn't read it.

What time is it?

Sir. You have the right to remain silent.

He just wanted to know how much time had been wasted.

They left the Driver behind.

He watched as the taxicab remained idle. Blocking two lanes. A variety of impatient horns coming from taxicabs and their drivers all more impatient than the one behind them.

The yellow glow hovered and froze.

There had been a clot.

The Customer was taken in to the nearest precinct.

19.

The Customer asked more questions than the detectives who wanted simply to know why. Everyone wants to know why.

The Customer didn't have a reply for any question that began with why.

He doesn't want to cooperate.

The Customer sat idly. Listening to the two detectives.

We can hold you here for questioning. You do know that?

Right?

Yes.

All we ask is why did you do it?

I still have my legs.

What the hell does that mean?

He fell right?

Who?

He fell and broke his legs.

Who are you thinking of?

I'm thinking of the same guy you're thinking of.

Look. We just want to know why. Why did you do it?

The Customer sat idly. Both detectives on the edge of their seats.

Fine.

The one with the temper left the room. He returned with one of the cops from before. They took him to a cell where they kept a number of other recent arrestees.

The Customer sat in the back idly.

No way to tell how much of the night's left.

The cell was bare minus the graffiti telling various tales of hate. Mostly hate.

You have to hate it all to end up here.

I did it.

The Customer looked to his right side. A large, muscular man was sitting next to him.

You did it huh.

Yeah. I did it. Not ashamed about it either. That racist motherfucker had it coming.

Yeah, he probably did.

You want to know why I did it. You probably want to know why I did it. It isn't hate.

There's a lot of hate on these walls.

Tell me about it. I respect public property. I respect people too. I have my reasons. Why I did it. You can't be pushed around. You know? You got to have self-confidence. You need to know your limits.

You can't take shit from people.

Damn right! You can't. The man's arms flexed whenever he stressed certain words. The Customer figured it wasn't voluntary. His body was after all connected to the mind. His body bulged with vigor. As if he had recently killed.

As if he recently shed violence.

He was prepped for me. It wouldn't take much to set him off.

The Customer sat there idly.

Everyone else sat on the other side of the cell. They were all maybe afraid.

You got to have your limits man!

Yes. I agree.

You have to show strength. Only the strong survive. That shit is real. We're animals and as animals the strongest survive. The strongest thrive!

Yes.

That's why I did it!

You had your reasons.

He misread me. I had to make it clear who I am. This is who I am. The man flexed both of his arms. One of the man's arms was as wide as the Customer's entire midsection. The guy said, Motherfucker had it coming!

The Customer sat idly.

There wasn't even the remote feeling of fear.

He wasn't afraid of this man. It calmed him sitting next to someone so heated and hated, someone that was looking at ten or maybe twenty years for crimes that he committed out of sheer need.

You got what you needed.

Damn right! The motherfucker will never walk again. I did it. I confess. You motherfuckers I did it! And I'll take my sentence thank you. The strongest will thrive. I'll rip anyone that so much as looks at me wrong into shreds. I'm a prison-lord in-the-making!

Jesus Christ… someone whispered to herself. She looked like she'd been on the street. She looked like a pro.

The man stood and confronted her. What did you say?!

Lay off the steroids. That's what I said.

I'm not on motherfucking steroids!

A cop banged his nightstick against the bars. Knock it off! You. The Customer looked at the cop. Yes. You! Come on.

Damn right I did it! Shouted the man. I'm the one. The one you looking for. I'm the killer showing my insides. He

grabbed at his crotch. I got the balls and I'm ready to show em. Bitch you ready to suck them?!

Okay that's enough! The cop pushed the Customer aside. You are free to go. The cop and two others entered the cell.

The Customer didn't see what happened next. He was already making his way out of the precinct.

He stopped to use the restroom.

When he left the restroom the muscular man was being manhandled by six cops. They were cuffing him at the wrists and ankles against a chair nailed down to the ground. The two detectives stood before him. They slammed the interrogation room shut. The cops remained inside the room. Just in case.

Such a sight might not be too difficult to understand.

People have their reasons.

They choose whatever shape they feel they need.

People separate and individualize themselves based on the shape they chose. Some need to be more intimidating. Some need to kill to satisfy a need.

It doesn't make anything easier.

In fact it makes everything worse.

Chasing happiness will get you nowhere.

It'll leave you a mess.

20.

If the Customer was just anybody else he would tell you that he didn't have a lot of aspirations as a kid. He just wanted to be confident and comfortable enough to not feel the way he does now.

He didn't want to wake up every morning reluctantly. That

same reluctance turned the whole waking-up process into one bloated episode of self-loathing. Daily routine. What would have been an hour at most getting ready took four hours. The whole morning. Just to get out of bed. Just to reach barely functional.

That was any morning. In a way if he were to commit suicide he'd be most prepared in the morning.

Botch suicide.

Try again.

That was the loathing way. There was no real loathing. Just perceived loathing. He was blank most times. These episodes were a mixture of acceptance and sheer disinterest.

He simply did not want to.

He wasn't interested.

Sometimes he couldn't fathom why people cared so much either.

It all seemed fruitless.

He felt sane enough. This was disengagement. That's all.

Whatever he had proposed had been proposed. There wasn't much else worth living for. And yet the mornings continued to arrive.

Nights were about as calm and tranquil as he could ever get.

Some nights it doesn't seem so bad. Then he realizes why he almost enjoys the night. The night often stirs up the trouble. By the time the trouble settles it feels, smells, and tastes like it might be the end.

It's so quiet at one specific section of the night you could easily pretend that you're the only one left alive.

Then morning comes and washes any glimmer away.

You're left as yourself.

A dedication to nothing.

21.

The Customer sat in the precinct lobby. Someone at reception said, Don't worry we'll call you a cab.

He looked outside as a cop pushed through the front doors.

A taxicab sat waiting.

He didn't react at first.

The Customer watched the cops and various employees of the precinct at work. It was almost calm. These crimefighters seemed like they had forgotten what crime really was. They were just people. This was a job.

And probably a shitty one.

When they arrested people they weren't arresting to serve and protect the law. Most of these cops did it out of spite.

At least they had their reasons.

The man with the muscles had his reasons.

The reasons led him here. A dead-end. Fast track to punishment. A man like that thrives on punishment. He loves punishing as much as being punished. Such a man perhaps enjoys the physical mess over the internal mess that never quite made sense to him. Any effort in trying to clear it up failed given how limited his brainpower was. He made up for it in muscle.

Physically clear.

The Customer walked to the cab. A number 7.

He got inside.

The Driver said, Are you good? Good. Yes?

He hesitated. This might be an even better use of the word confusing. The Customer was confused. He brushed it aside. The Customer nodded.

Good. Good. We go. Yes. I take you. We go.

The Customer looked out his window. Inside a black SUV someone was watching him. He couldn't make out the face but he made out the flashing of a camera. That someone then glared at him.

The Customer glared back.

There was history hidden in these strange paranoid waves.

No tension. No dread. The taxicab drove off.

The Driver as usual did all the talking.

The night is young, said the Driver. Much to go. Much to see. We go.

22.

Three cars followed at random intervals. The taxicab managed to keep the same pace and for a while the Customer felt as though they were making up for lost and wasted time.

They were taking back the night.

This was a journey.

Journey to staying with the night.

He had a few back-ups in case it didn't work.

He could get lost in the alleys of the city.

It's never anything but night in those alleys. Neither sun nor time affects what stews, molds and mutates in the city's alleys.

But that was a back-up. For now the Driver kept assuring him he was taking him somewhere.

The Customer was beginning to believe him.

The followers remained at a distance. Just distant enough to maybe be brushed off as imagination.

There'd be on occasion a stranger running down the street.

The stranger would stop short and glare at the taxicab as it passed. Like the taxicab had stolen something from the stranger. The look was one of disbelief.

The city was after something.

But what?

23.

The taxicab passed by one of the most popular media centers in the city and the Customer observed that they were setting up a gallery opening. The gallery opening occurred at precisely seven. This meant it couldn't be any later than six thirty.

The Customer noticed the discrepancy.

It couldn't be that early.

Time slows and it speeds up.

But the night was gripping hold.

The Customer asked that question:

Why?

The Driver replied, I take you.

A kind of question nobody really could answer.

24.

The Customer drifted into what wasn't quite sleep.

He was younger.

Young enough to be anything he wanted to be.

If only he had the means. And he had the means.

He was one of the white-collar.

The Customer was always the customer. The one receiving.

He could pay because his family could pay.

And he was off to college. Things progressed quickly during these times.

He hadn't really wanted to but he also didn't put up much of a fight like his siblings did. They wanted original lives.

Mother said you should be what you want to be.

Father said you have to do what you have to do.

A brother would say you're a piece of shit. Never amount to anything.

A sister would say you could be better if you'd stop being a dork.

After leaving it was like he didn't have any family.

He was off on his own.

A lump sum to get started. Now go.

That was the way.

He got things going and it wasn't that he was happy. He was just busy. Too busy to think about much of anything else. Work was work.

Work was all.

During down points, which were mostly holidays, he got a taste of what he'd feel before feeling nothing.

He drifted off to somewhere because home had been cut up into slices. Each sibling took their share and mother and father separated. Finally. It was a long time coming. One time he drifted back to their childhood home.

What was called home.

It was some other family's home. They were nice enough to invite him to their Thanksgiving holiday. He accepted before realizing that they were just being courteous.

He ruined their holiday with awkward vibes and broken conversations.

It was a mess.

He stopped drifting. He focused on work.

Work became something and it gave as much as work could give. Dollar signs and plenty of affairs but nothing specific. Nothing meaningful.

He was lacking what the other businessmen seemed to have: a goal.

But you keep working and things work out.

Everything works out except for what can't be easily handled.

When you're like him you don't have much of an afternoon to waste but the night comes forward for a twelve round boxing match with your emotions.

By the twelfth year the twelfth round he doesn't feel much.

He works out of routine. He runs on that routine. When it finally shatters he realizes there's too much to clean up and no real motivation to do so.

He leaves the hotel where he had arrived the night before with no intention of returning. He ends up in a taxicab with nowhere to go.

He doesn't want to move forward.

He doesn't want to go back.

Whenever he goes back it ends up more fragmented than the last time he visited. Soon it'll be a single haymaker to the face and he'll wake up with a headache.

The taxicab sped over a few potholes which caused the cabin to rattle. The Customer woke up. It seemed he had slept. He rubbed at his eyes. Tried his hardest to regain consciousness.

It really felt like he had been in a boxing match.

Exhaustion gripped him tight. Then he realized they were going in circles.

The Driver was waiting for the Customer to wake up.

Good. Good. Now we go. The Driver expertly crossed three clogged lanes in only a few feet and parallel parked the taxicab.

The Customer looked up at the sign.

It was all the same letter. The letter X.

25.

Why are we here, is a question the Customer asked the Driver and the Driver replied, Friend. We meet. We talk. I have friend. He helps.

The Driver misunderstood him. It was more complicated than that.

It was a question to stop all the other questions.

The Customer wanted the Driver to stop talking and to start driving again.

26.

The friend doesn't help. The friend is simply someone that peeks into every fissure in the city looking for leads and lingering opportunities to pounce and exploit.

The friend isn't mastermind of this porn empire. The friend is a customer just like everyone else.

Inside this place the Customer is almost instantly used to the smell, managing to stomach the first couple gags.

The Driver doesn't go inside. The Driver doesn't say why or maybe it's that the Driver can't put it into words. You go. I

stay. Stay with the cab. The cab.

Okay.

The Customer hasn't been here before. At least he doesn't think so.

No.

Not this one.

He's been to another.

These little porn empires are the last specks of face-to-face perversion in a world where pornography of all kinds is more easily found via websites and other snatch programs.

Go here to get your fix of naked flesh.

The friend is here to do just that.

The Customer didn't find the friend. The friend found the Customer.

He sat him down in one of the jerk-off booths.

The smell.

The lingering urge to not-touch-anything.

The friend is saying in equally broken English but somehow better than the Driver's that he can take him away from this place.

I can find. Yes. I can find what you cannot find.

Okay, said the Customer.

I look into you and I see you need away. Away from here. I can get you away from here. Will you let me, yes?

The Customer sat idly.

The friend acted very much like a friend but what he was trying to do was sell the Customer on the service of stowing him away.

Getting him out of this city. This country. Somewhere else.

But what made any other city, any other country, better than the one where he has at the very least memorized its

layout, its mannerisms, its messes?

The friend offered an example.

One hell of a satisfied customer.

The friend it turns out is a friend to the Driver at the very least.

The Driver is here strictly because of this friend.

He happy, yes?

Yes.

Very happy. Big man in the city he has time of his life. You can be having time of your life too. I can help. I am friend. A friend for those that need. And you need.

The Customer looks around the place. Booths filled. Booths open for-the-taking. A few naked women with butt plugs lodged up their rectums from previous clients wander around looking to sell their orifices a few more times before they become too sore.

Men file in and find their kicks. They get going and soon they too are wandering around with erect penises looking for holes to plow into.

This is an empire. A thriving and throbbing empire.

This can only be possible in the city.

The friend is talking. The Customer isn't listening.

I sell happiness. Is what I do. Yes. I can make it good. The friend's chief product isn't making waves so he moves on to yet another. The friend is a seller and reseller of what no one in their right mind needs. He only sells what they think they need. And most of the time that kind ends up hurting them.

You can make it good, said the Customer.

Yes. I can make it very good.

Okay.

How much you want?

How much happiness do I want.

Yes. Yes. How much?

You can measure happiness?

Yes. Look. How much. The dosage. It don't last long. You buy a lot.

I can buy a lot of happiness.

Yes! Good. Only the rich can buy happiness. You rich. Very rich.

Actually I am not rich.

As it turns out he isn't much of a friend at all.

You can't pay?

No I can't pay.

Profanities in his native language. Get out!

This isn't your booth.

Get out! Get out!

I'll get out. The Customer steps out of the booth and is faced with an empire that might have no real living owner. Such empires are often godless.

The Customer has, like in most situations, two main choices:

Stay or leave.

The Customer can hear moaning in the distance. Upon further inspection it's coming from a speaker right above him.

The moment for leaving passes.

It looks like he's staying.

27.

They don't know the meaning of night in this place. He's never ventured down these halls before. Outside the taxicab and the Driver are nowhere to be seen.

He's been left behind.

The Customer apparently looks like a customer.

They are all wanting to treat him right. Men. Women. Men and/or women with animals. Men and other men. Women and a lot of other women.

The digital screen.

Operators with machinery.

A tired face telling him there's toys and other things in the back.

A man with wide eyes whispering into his ear as he passes:

Don't take the next right. Just don't.

The hall is draped in darkness.

Not a soul in sight.

28.

The Customer found a woman that wasn't like the rest. Or really the woman found him. And she wasn't at all like the rest.

She told him so.

She tells him often.

They walk the empire together. Don't hold her hand.

Don't look into her eyes.

These are her rules.

A policy perhaps. The Customer isn't about to do what he's been told not to do. He doesn't want another mess of a situation.

Right about now he can only stomach what is simple and understandable.

Nothing better jump out at him.

He won't so much as wince.

The Customer is incapable of reaction.

If the danger is deadly, consider him dead.

He won't even so much as blink.

He'll take it.

Once more.

They wandered through those halls, took that right turn.

The Customer looked to the ceiling. It was missing.

You could see the wiring.

At his feet roaches scurried with them in such dense patches that it looked more like the floor was moving.

A used condom moved on its own, resting on the backs of the roaches.

Along for the ride.

Everyone's looking for a ride.

She told him this.

They reached yet another fork. Left. Straight. Or Right.

He couldn't see down any of these halls.

Blind faith.

They went straight.

Put your faith in me. Is what she said.

They reached a set of rooms side by side.

Rooms without anything in them. Unpainted. Missing doors.

No windows.

She walked into one of the rooms.

He followed.

A room with no purpose.

This will do just fine.

She took her clothes off.

He kept his on.

She didn't have a scratch on her. Silky smooth skin.

You don't belong here. You look at me like I'm something to covet rather than consume. This is what she tells him.

The Customer didn't so much as sigh.

She said a lot more before he had his way with her. To be more precise before she had her way with him.

The end result was uneventful. Meaning nothing happened.

But she could talk.

And based solely on what she said it was an open book.

It sounded like the most precious and perverted thing any two people could do to each other without having it end in a pool of their own blood.

This is what she said.

29.

Talk to me. Tell me everything. Tell me lies. My ears are yours. And so is my body. Every part of me.

Yours.

Find yourself in me.

And tell it you still care.

I've shaved. Look. I'm waxed and clean.

I am not a mess.

I am easy.

I am what you don't know you need.

Talk to me.

I'll let you do anything.

Anything.

I will be right here. Talk.

Talk.

Talk to me.

Please. Talk. Say something.

Speak.

The Customer stood idly.

I'm all words as long as you can perform. But please tell me first. Tell me your name.

Tell me something.

Something that only you could say.

Tell me. No one is listening.

It's only me.

I'll be anything you want me to be.

The Customer asked, Is this how you usually work?

Why? Do I look like I'm beautiful?

You look beautiful.

Do I look like I'm made up to work with the rest of these women?

You look like you like working here.

I don't work here. I have been asked. I have even been told that I work here. But I don't work here. I am beautiful.

Why can't I be satisfied and be myself at the same time?

Because you're a whore, replied the Customer.

You can say anything to me. Anything. If I'm a whore you're a slut.

We will be as we are here. Right now. We are simply getting what we need. This is not love.

I can take you home.

If you want me to.

I can. If you're inside my home you ought to know that I trust you.

I'll let you do anything to me.

I can do anything, replied the Customer.

You are mine. I am yours. You could walk me like a dog around the park. I'll let you. You could hang me high and try and kill me.

I will let you.

But it isn't love. To be touched you have to be in love. You have to care.

I don't care, replied the Customer.

I don't care about you.

I only want you to fuck me. I want to fuck you.

I need you to talk to me.

I don't love you, replied the Customer.

She was naked. She touched herself and had a taste.

This was more for effect.

She wanted him home with her.

She wanted him right then and there.

He told her she looked clean.

She assured him that she was in every way.

They stood in silence and then left the room.

They wandered down the hall. She went first.

The Customer didn't observe her shapely curves. She had a fully waxed body. Every limb. Every crevice. She was as clean as a doll. On the outside.

He didn't look at her full ass.

When she stopped to pick something up he didn't catch a glimpse of her. He didn't note how she was barefoot. Soles of her feet black and being scratched by the broken beer bottle shards and other refuse.

They reached an area of activity in the empire.

A naked woman wasn't anything uncommon.

She gained a few glances while he kept walking.

He could hear her calling. She wasn't calling to him. He could hear her say familiar words. I'm not like the rest. She was saying. And don't bother touching me. She was saying. I have something to tell you.

She was saying to somebody else.

The Customer kept walking.

Outside he flagged down a taxicab.

The number on the side was the lowest yet.

He got into the number 1.

You're everywhere all at once, said the Customer.

Yes. Hello. Yes.

The Driver started talking. My apologies. Friend. My many many apologies. I take you. I have better. Much better. My friends are many friends.

You have a lot of friends, said the Customer.

Yes. Yes. We go. I take you.

30.

Between the few moments it took for the Driver to tell the Customer that it was barely midnight and pulling the taxicab back into the yellow glow of the city's veins, the Customer noticed a woman standing near an alley smoking a clove.

You don't usually think much of these sightings unless they are of a rarer variety. The shadows pouring out of the alley made it impossible to get a good look at her but it was obvious:

This was one of those sightings.

She took a long drag and held it in.

She exhaled a pale smoke. The smoke covered her face. Her eyes pierced through. She was watching as if saying, I am watching you.

I don't love you, is what he said. Of course nobody was there to hear this. They were hollow words used to make it

seem like he was saying something in response to the woman's intrusion upon his sense of privacy.

There was nobody to love.

Only a bunch of people looking to get something from you and in return you maybe get something back.

Everybody needs something. The greedy ones want a bit more.

Plenty of greed to keep you punch-drunk.

The Customer kept quiet as the Driver started repeating the same broken phrases of apology. Apparently hours had passed since the Customer entered the porn empire. What a waste of time.

Hurling down the road he caught a glimpse of the woman.

She had something in her hands. A flash and he knew.

Was it something he did or said?

They were taking pictures of him like he wouldn't be there for much longer. The woman wasn't the first and definitely wasn't the last.

There was value to catching a glimpse of the Customer.

31.

The taxicab was in motion. The Driver was taking the Customer to an entirely different part of the city. You usually need to have a past to call this place possible. Possible to gain access. And yet the Driver breezed on by gate after gate. There was absolutely no hesitation on either part.

The Driver. The Customer.

They couldn't be any different.

Maybe they were precisely the same.

It was one of those moments.

The kind where both knew it would be awhile before they reached their next destination. This was a good time to talk.

They could find out how similar they were. Maybe the stereotype was true and they were entirely different. Maybe.

Their differences might help the both of them better understand what they were and what they weren't in their own lives.

One of those conversations where it would start out with a cough.

A clearing of the throat.

One of them saying, Where are you from?

Then a response.

Finding a place. Getting a feel for the setting.

Telling stories.

One of them saying, How did you… and then maybe trail off.

Maybe that was an actual question.

Maybe there is an actual reply.

The awkward exchange would remain sharp. They couldn't get comfortable with each other as anything other than Driver and Customer.

Customer isn't required to give a name.

Driver gives no name.

No whys are given.

The conversation in theory surrounds this grandiose need to relate to each other. The Driver having been the driver all this night. The Customer having continued to remain idle. An open book that's blank.

However there was no conversation.

The Driver found it too difficult to say anything other

than the maybe two dozen phrases he had memorized for the job. Things like, Yes. I take you. We go. Friend. No. And street names. The entire map of the city including the small fine print under the map's legend. Read this. Memorize this. Where to?

Don't drive until dawn.

Stay with the night.

32.

Yellow glow punctuated by marauding clots of shimmering chrome. Those damn trucks. Yellow. Jet black. Yellow. Jet Black. Inside one of these is a single mind at work behind her laptop.

Fingers fluttering away.

That ruckus. The keyboard tap-tapping.

The Customer, he can almost hear it.

Imagine that he can.

Might drive him mad. So keep going. And please tomorrow don't come.

The Driver puts up a veritable defense with his talking. Rambling limited talking. Assumed the Customer is listening.

And fine. He'd rather listen to this than remember what hides where he cannot see. Waiting. Keeping track. Marking. Taking pictures.

Taking detailed notes.

So that if the question why ever comes up he's a perfect example.

He's not just anybody. He's the Customer. With a capital C.

But where the Driver takes him that polluted yellow glow of the city full of potential danger and unwanted obligation streaks thin.

In some stretches it's as safe as the darkest of night.

In some stretches it seems to make sense.

The night lives here.

33.

They pulled up behind the taxicab. They forced the Driver to pull off the road. Nothing but the night out there.

Two men per SUV stepped out of their respective seats.

The Driver said, You know? Do you? Do you know?

The Customer sat idly.

He didn't say anything. Not even a word.

One of the men approached the taxicab.

The man tapped on the glass.

The Driver rolled down the window from his seat. Some of these taxicabs are better equipped than you think. Not all of them are falling to pieces.

The yellow gets you where you need to go.

And sometimes where you don't.

The man peeked into the backseat. Sir. Enough is enough. You're more than half an hour late. You know how the fans don't like to be kept waiting.

Yeah. The fans don't like to be kept waiting.

They are your fans. Sir. Sir? Now please. The man tried to open the door but the Driver had locked all the doors. The man looked in the direction of the driver's seat.

Tell the cabbie to unlock the doors.

The Driver was talking to him and to the man at once using the same few lines. We go. No. Not this man. You celebrity? Why don't you feel happy?

The Customer said to the man, Not a cabbie. My driver.

Sure. Sure whatever. But we're wasting time.

We are wasting time, said the Customer, his stomach sinking.

Is that daylight in the distance? But no. It was just his eyes and imagination playing tricks on him.

Then let's go. We can't move until you do.

The men returned to their cars. They drove to the front, side and rear of the taxicab and forced the Driver to keep to their speed and to follow them deeper into the city.

Deeper into the darkness until little sparkles of synthetic light flickered to life. The Driver saw it first and said, There. We go there. Where they take us?

The Customer replied, Yeah. I think I know where they're taking us.

34.

Boxed in, the taxicab is the opposite of freedom. Boxed in, the Driver isn't really driving. Boxed in, the taxicab isn't going anywhere. Boxed in, the Driver is just like his customer.

This upsets the Driver.

A moment of escalating anger.

Certainly there's a lot that could be said.

Yes. Yes.

Certainly. But there wouldn't be anybody there to say it to.

And even if they could hear the Driver, they wouldn't be able to understand him. In order for the Driver to be able to express himself he speaks in his native language. The language barrier makes it hard for the Customer to understand really anything the Driver might say.

These words are not to be spoken.

The Driver spoke.

Driver isn't just an empty canvas. He said it aloud.

The Customer sat idly in the backseat.

He looked straight ahead.

The Driver looked straight ahead.

The only difference between the both of them was that his mouth was moving while the Customer's was a thin line glued closed.

It is not my problem.

My problem is my fare. My problem is my cab. This is mine.

My problem is where I shall take my customer.

The Customer.

It is my problem that he has asked and I've told him that I can. That I can take him. If he wants to. And he wants to. So I will take him.

These men are making it difficult.

The SUVs were slowing to a crawl. Eventually the vehicles stopped.

The Customer got out of the taxicab.

The Customer could not show up in a taxicab.

The men were making it obvious to both Driver and Customer that they would be taking over. They would be making sure he gets to where they want him to go. The Driver twisted his grip on the steering wheel.

A waste of time. Yes. This is waste. No good.

The Driver watched as the Customer got into one of the SUVs.

The SUVs left the taxicab parked in the right lane. Just out of sight the Driver heard a loud screeching. The obvious sound of tires.

A moment later the three SUVs were sighted speeding in the opposite direction back towards where they had come. Back towards the city.

The Driver said aloud, No good.

Heading in that direction they were already two hours too late.

35.

In the cushioned and overly comfortable backseat of the SUV the Customer sat idly as usual. One man drove while the other sat in the front passenger seat.

Seemed like an easy gig.

The man that wasn't driving said, He isn't real right?

The Customer replied, I don't know.

Afterwards everybody was silent.

Sometimes there's nothing to say.

The only thing to do is drive.

This was one of those occasions.

They were barreling down the street.

Not that it would matter much.

Ten. Twenty. Thirty miles over the speed limit.

No matter how quickly they drove they couldn't make up for lost time.

In their case it was forty-five over the speed limit.

36.

The men soon forgot about the Customer when it turned out

the one they were looking for had arrived at the venue and had already begun the selling and signing of books. The men made a mistake.

Nobody wanted to stick around after making a mistake.

The Customer walked into the venue. Some center for emerging media. A fancy name for a store that sells whatever's new in film and literature and videogames and anything escapist.

People call it entertainment.

The author looked nothing like the Customer.

The line wrapped around the entire store and spilled out onto the street. Sucks to be those people waiting in line outside. By the time they reached the author he would have been replaced with another author. They'd have to buy this author's book and pretend like they were here to meet him and not the former.

The Customer ignored the line and walked forward to the desk where the author sat. The author nodded and grinned and posed right on cue.

The men had left him here. They drove off fearing their error would be the end of their jobs.

Might as well meet the author. The man of the moment. The dawn to his dusk. The person that looked nothing like him but the men had figured they were identical. Exactly alike.

He stood to the left of the author. Not in line. Not speaking.

He stood and watched the signing.

The author's fans gushing. Faces red. Some tearing up. Others demanding a hug or a picture. Adulation.

This was not love.

The author hadn't noticed him standing there and yet he

begun talking to him. He talked to him like nobody else was listening. The fans eavesdropped but acted as though the author really valued their time and their support.

The line never stops you know.

I know, replied the Customer.

They keep coming until I can't write any more and then I'm done. Washed up. Burnt out.

It happens to everybody.

Yeah of course. It happened to that guy over there.

There was a man sitting in one of the reading chairs. His hands were folded so tightly as if frozen in prayer. His hands appeared to be melded together into one grip. His face was buried in a book.

He's trying to find his voice.

Another writer. The one that started this whole thing. She's in line. She's the one with the shit-eating grin, huge bloodshot eyes that drip tears like she's a disaster.

The Customer looked around. He couldn't find her.

That girl over there. The platinum blonde hair. Thin like scratch marks.

The Customer saw her. She was maybe fifty people back. The line started to inch closer and she got out of line and squeezed back in something like five or ten people back.

Yeah. She doesn't want to meet me. She's having trouble coping. Moving on from this. Some people are dreamers. They don't aspire to get what they need to survive. They only want what they want. When they don't get it there's nothing to do but snap.

The Customer picked up a copy of the author's book. $34.99.

He said, Prestige is expensive.

Yeah. Well not my fault. It's the publisher. Hardcovers are a bitch and a half to print and sell. Prestige is my latest. For every one person that recognizes your name they add thirty cents to the price tag.

The Customer set the book down without reading the synopsis.

Doesn't seem very successful does it? You are probably thinking: Why seize it when there's no movement, no motivation? And when nothing is worth holding, why is it so wrong to sit down, idly, for a while. A long while.

That's not what I was thinking.

Well I've told my agent and I've told the publisher. I can't keep this up for much longer. Eventually nobody will read me. I'll be a closed book.

The author showed his teeth. He shook a fan's hand. The fan said stuff like how much he loved this book and that book and how he thinks that the author is getting better with every book but he then tempers the ass-kissing with some unoriginal criticism. The fan said that a lot of his books were the same stories and same types of characters. The writing has gotten better but everything else has stayed the same. The author had an answer to every little bit of witticism and criticism.

He kept that smile picture-perfect and as sharp as can be.

The fan seemed satisfied and paid for Prestige. $34.99. The fan was lucky because in ten to fifteen more fans the price was going up $44.99.

Right before I write my last sentences the price will be $49.99. I get maybe ten percent of that. But that's why I'm three people.

The Customer observed the line of fans. It was lengthening. The clerks and supervisors of the store were starting another line on the opposite side of the street. The city was pouring in

and you could hear it.

You could see the yellow taxicab glow.

It was getting harder to see the author.

He was still talking of course. The Customer tuned in and out at various times. In his periphery the Customer saw a young female face. She looked familiar. Black eyeliner. Use of subculture fashion. Expressionless face. She held a pen in her hand. She was the author's replacement.

The author was way ahead of everybody else.

He was busy pre-signing books.

He said, He isn't real is he?

The Customer looked down the line of fans to the curb outside.

There was a taxicab parked. A number 3.

You couldn't see the Driver but of course the Customer expected the Driver to be behind the wheel. Ready to take him away.

To keep up with the night.

It was getting late.

How did the author know?

The Customer replied, No he isn't real.

The author chuckled, Now look who's counting the messes.

The young girl stood behind the author waiting to replace him.

He wasn't saying any goodbyes. Instead he was using the time left to confess what he's done. I'm not like this book here. I'm not a liar.

I needed the prestige. Sure. I did. I thought I did.

I paid my way instead of letting it be paved by hard work. I mean I worked. Sure. I worked hard. But you get into this mode. This competitive mode where you're trying to get your

life together. What I ask is the question that can't be asked because nobody can answer it. Why? Why get a life together? And what the hell is a life anyway?

I've met fans that bought my books at truck stops. They live on the road. They pay for gas and food and free time with the skills they've acquired. They fix peoples' cars. They drive a truck halfway across the country.

They live day to day because that's life. That's the bare minimum.

It's the only requirement. The only thing we all need to do on a daily basis is survive. Anything that's above making sure you are fed and are feeling fine isn't worth a damn. It's excess. That's prestige.

I could have summed the entire book up in just a few rants. Instead I made some story up of some guy who has it all and flushes it and then finds it again. Finds some kind of philosophical meaning. Something that everybody believes is waiting for them. Nothing is in wait. This is only living.

That's it.

The author turned around and looked up at the young face.

He turned back towards the Customer and said:

I'm a dot. Now watch how effortlessly I disappear.

37.

Inside the taxicab the Driver is speaking in his own language.

The Customer listens to the Driver's words.

The taxicab makes up for wasted time.

How late is it?

How much of the night is left?

Has the night left him behind?

The Driver is taking him somewhere. Back towards the darkness just beyond the city. Where gates require pass codes to open.

They are taking a familiar road.

That road.

No sign of the SUVs.

The Customer sat idly. The Driver wasn't talking.

Both were in balance.

They both enjoyed the drive.

38.

There is a shifting of the night. All of a sudden the air feels thicker. The movement slower and yet more precise.

A whiff of car exhaust. Dread?

39.

The taxicab pulled up to a gate with a pretty floral design. The taxicab was buzzed in without the Driver having to even roll the window down to request entry.

The Driver pulled the taxicab up to the front of an impressive estate. This house sparkled with serenity and a peaceful atmosphere made possible by high-end architectural design.

The Driver said, You go. I wait.

The Customer got out of the taxicab.

The taxicab drove off.

The Driver had somewhere to be.

40.

There you are! The woman sat on the front balcony sizing him up from afar.

She came from another time. She haunted a previous life.

Those red eyes. How could he forget?

She jumped to her feet and ran towards him. Grabbed him by the hand like a young girl and together they went into the house.

The house was as immaculately decorated as the outside.

Do you like what I've done to the place?!

Her bubbling personality. How could he forget.

He forgot her until now.

Him and her. Her and him. They had shared a first kiss.

A first embrace.

A childhood.

You wouldn't believe how much I spent getting this place to feel like home! The architect didn't design this place for a homey feel. My husband's friend is an architect you see. He's ambitious. He designed this place as a showpiece. He designs every house to be a showpiece.

She gave him the tour. Room to room.

The would-be bedroom of her son. Her would-be daughter. The would-be guest room. The three empty rooms. Her room or the would-be master's bedroom of a husband and wife.

My husband is a busy man. He's gone a lot away on business.

So you can see why I need the house to really feel like home.

I need it to feel like me. Like it's a part of me.

This is my world!

Where do you live?

I live in the city, replied the Customer.

The city! My my! You must be doing well for yourself!

I am well.

Why I've forgotten what the city looks like. The city seems so far away from here…

The basement.

The party room complete with billiards, an untouched bar, and a number of video arcade machines.

A number of other rooms.

The kitchen.

She pointed outside. The maid's house.

The maid does such a great job keeping this place clean but she doesn't speak a word of English. I really wish she did. To think, the one person I see on a daily basis won't even speak to me.

She sat him down in a room full of couches and mirrors.

This is the mirror room. I like sitting here and thinking.

I feel like a philosopher when I sit in this room.

She grinned. Those red eyes of hers glowed.

How are you?

He replied, I am fine.

Perhaps she wanted him to ask her the same thing but he didn't and so she had to cough twice and say, I'm doing well too.

Remember in fourth grade when you and I were in gym class and they were picking teams for dodge ball. You were obviously going to be picked first and I was picked last but you refused to leave my side until I was picked. You were always at my side…

He was supposed to say something here.

He didn't.

She took out a bunch of pictures. Seven in all.

I've kept what I couldn't keep as memory. Here's us when were seven or eight years old playing on that old tire swing.

She handed him the picture.

And this picture was of that one time. I forgot whose birthday party it was but remember we ended up giving that person the same gift?

She handed him the picture.

Oh. This one. I think you remember this one. I forgot who it was that took the photo. Who was with us when you gave me my first kiss?

She handed him the picture.

She laughed. You were always so silly. How many cigarettes are you smoking in this picture?

She handed him the picture.

My sister always had a thing for you. She took a lot of photos of you whenever we'd go swimming. This one time she managed to take a photo of you naked when we skinny dipped that one summer. She ruined her camera in the process but she got it. I'm glad I found it.

She handed him the picture.

She sighed. I must say I wish it was you and not him. You two were best-of-friends. What happened? I don't believe I fell in love with him. I fell in love with you first.

She handed him the picture.

Well then. This is a surprise. I don't recall seeing you at our wedding.

She handed him the picture.

My favorite. Your mom took this picture of us the second time I spent the night. We were young. Five or six. We stayed

up all night watching cartoons and eating ice cream. It was probably one of the happiest moments of my life.

She handed him the picture.

The pictures were all of the same thing. They depicted the Customer sitting in the backseat of a taxicab. The number on the side of the taxi changed with each picture but it was nearly a copy. A copy of a copy. A copy of countless other copies. Same blank expression on his face. Same angle. Same lighting.

They were pictures of him attempting to flee.

41.

They sipped gourmet coffee as she brought him up to speed. Her husband. His former high school friend. The guy had found success in the stock market. That coupled with his father dying from cancer and the inherited lump sum got him started on the greed-filled journey into venture capitalism.

The guy was doing well for himself.

She had become a bit of a trophy wife.

Because he was worth thirty million she was worth thirty million.

She mentioned how she once tried to buy herself happiness.

No matter how much she bought she couldn't get addicted.

The effects wore off an hour or two later.

It made her tired.

Happiness was a loose end. A little cutting and voila: No more.

She slept off happiness until she was back into her jovially repressed state. There was a lot of talk about teaching the maid to speak English.

It didn't happen but she took a few courses in the maid's native language trying to find a middle ground.

It seemed the maid didn't want to speak to her.

The distance was comforting.

Then she started talking about him and her. The love that was.

In her case the love that still might be.

But she had to take it all back just as soon as she said it. Had to.

She loved her husband.

I love him.

I do.

I love him.

She said all she needed in life was love.

But it didn't sound very convincing. She had to explain herself.

I used to have no way of explaining what it was that makes me feel and act this way… but I'm getting better. I am. I… I've been wondering if the love I need isn't enough. Love itself isn't enough.

And I've had nightmares about this but I know I can trust you and I need to tell someone… I really do. I need to say it.

I have wondered if I need love at all…

I don't need it…

Again she didn't sound very convincing.

Then she's breaking down and asking for forgiveness.

She asks him for a kiss. One more kiss.

There is talk about how she pays people to find and follow her past.

She isn't asking for love.

That's not what she needs.

In fact… she doesn't know what she needs.

And he isn't going to help her.

Everyone's trying to clean themselves up. Clean themselves up as if to be sold or resold for hopefully an equal or higher price.

Sell me?

Sell me one kiss. Please.

But he doesn't want any money.

She's left looking at herself from a number of angles. The mirrors reflect what she's missing: The love for herself. That kind of love is something a person really needs. Care for yourself or you can't stand it.

Every minute is anguish.

Shattering glass can be heard as the Customer exits the house.

42.

The Driver is approximately five or six miles down the road at the only gas station in this particular area of the suburbs.

The taxicab is parked at the number 5 pump and he's leaning maybe dozing while the tank is being filled.

Another taxicab pulls up. A number 12.

The other driver gets out of his cab and does the same.

They eventually glance at each other.

Both drivers speak.

They speak the same language. To them it isn't the language of a foreign country. It's the language of the road. A language shared by drivers not customers.

The Driver is saying, What a mess.

The other driver replies, Yes. Such a big mess.

The Driver peeks into the backseat of the other driver's taxicab.

The Driver asks, He real?

The other driver replies, What do you think?

They finish filling up their taxicabs and then nod to each other.

And just like that they are back on the road. Blending in with the yellow glow. Keeping with the flow of traffic.

Keeping with the night.

A destination clear in mind. Dictated by the Customer.

43.

The Customer was in the backseat trying his damnedest not to fall asleep. It was getting late or at least felt like it. The Driver observed the Customer in his rearview mirror.

Music? said the Driver.

The Customer asked. What time is it?

The Driver spoke to him in a different language.

The Customer wasn't supposed to understand him but he did. And maybe it was because the Driver wanted him to understand.

You keep asking the time. What does it matter? I mean come on man. We've been driving around all night. What have you found?

Really? What have you found that makes anything any better?

Can you relate to them?

Can anybody relate to anybody?

I don't think you want or need anything else. Why can't you let me do the driving? Let me do the driving.

Forget about the time. I can't drive if you keep asking me the same things.

So sit and stay calm.

Let me drive.

Let's… just enjoy the drive. Okay?

The Customer relaxed. He was no longer sleepy.

44.

The secret actions of the city recede and become yet again the nothingness between monuments and buildings of residence and business. There are people inside these buildings and inside these homes. They are finishing up their offering. Their day's effort.

They are tying up loose ends.

Calling family and friends. They spray out like bloody vapor into the streets. Many of them hustle trying to keep up the pace they've kept so far.

It's that time.

Night is arriving.

It's time to give up for the day.

The day is over.

It's time to maybe have some fun.

How many of those are wasted? How many of those are absorbed?

45.

He grabbed at his cellphone. A number of missed calls. He

had no intention of returning any of them. He looked at the time on his phone.

He checked to see how much battery life was left.

The Driver turned on the radio.

It was a familiar song.

The Customer looked outside the window.

People outside cluttered the streets.

They were all busy making plans. What to do tonight.

The Driver switched lanes. He took a right at one particular street.

The number so high it either wrapped back around to Main Street or stood to transform into an entirely different street.

A street with a new name. Not a number.

The taxicab has no one in front of it and no one behind it. It speeds up.

The street ahead is cast in the calming darkness of night.

The shadows are nearly impenetrable.

The street narrows into a one-lane passage. To some extent it looks more like an alley than a street.

The Driver reaches under the dashboard

Safety is kept close.

The Customer closes his eyes.

Places trust in the only person that doesn't know his name.

He intends on enjoying the drive.

Wherever it might take him.

The Driver says in a different language:

The night is young.

46.

I am a mess.

FLIP TO
SIDE B TO
CONTINUE
READING